Healer's Twilight

Blent Hurd

Healer's Twilight

Blant Hurt

Writer's Showcase
presented by *Writer's Digest*
San Jose New York Lincoln Shanghai

Healer's Twilight

Writer's Showcase
presented by *Writer's Digest*
an imprint of iUniverse.com, Inc.

For information address:
iUniverse.com, Inc.
5220 S 16th, Ste. 200
Lincoln, NE 68512
www.iuniverse.com

ISBN: 0-595-14100-5

Printed in the United States of America

CHAPTER I

The medical center in Madsen emerged from nothing in the 1920s: from converted houses that held only ten beds, from a five-hundred-acre plot of fallow land, and from the will and vision of the townspeople. The first patients were locals in for yellow fever vaccinations, hare lips, cleft palates. Through the decades, medicine progressed, but at few places anywhere did it advance as rapidly and impressively as at the medical center. In the 1960s, European royalty came here for treatment from the best doctors. Now, the medical center and the town surrounding it had grown into an affluent city.

David Heyworth was a heart surgeon at Mercy Hospital. He and his four staffers occupied a suite of rooms in an adjacent building. In Heyworth's own small office, leather chairs faced each side of his L-shaped desk. Tall bookcases were filled with medical textbooks and Sir James Osler's histories of heart surgery and back issues of The Annals of Thoracic Surgery. The bookends were bronzed busts of ancient doctors—Hippocrates, Galen, Pasteur, Maimonides, Roentgen—and on a lower bookshelf was a needlepoint pillow, sewn for him by his mother when he was in his early twenties. The inscription read: "Maybe in error. Never in doubt."

The doctor's green eyes, deep-set and riveting, conveyed intelligence and a constant, vigilant awareness, and his hair was gray-black like a thundercloud and neatly clipped. He was as careful and determined about his appearance as he was in his work.

On his great desk was a citation, a complaint, from the hospital's Quality Assurance department. The heavy black letters across the bottom of the page read: Occurrence: Fluid Overload in Patient. "Dammit," Heyworth said loudly to himself. "Dammit, that's enough already!"

Out in the hallway, Constance heard him and came in. She was long-limbed and plain-featured, and she managed Heyworth's office so competently that when she missed a workday, he felt disorganized. "What?" she said in her two-syllabled drawl.

"Read this." He thrust the citation at her. "This letter's one of the most maddening things I've seen around this hospital lately."

Constance looked at the yellow page, then back up at Heyworth's face, watching his expression closely because she judged her job performance according to the mood he was in.

"Do they mean Mr. Ettinger drank too much water?" he said. "That he got too much IV fluid? Exactly what do they mean by this?"

"Beats me. The patient didn't have any post-op problems last week, did he?"

"No. Yet this citation is written as if he had some horrendous complication involving fluids. Let me see it again."

He snatched the page from her and looked at it, his eyes squinted. Then he swiveled in his chair to the big window, staring beyond the weekly schedule that Constance had taped there. The sky was pale blue, burdened with humidity. From his tenth-floor office, his gaze dropped to the tree-line spreading westward over the flat land. This view typically made him feel optimistic, but now his brow wrinkled.

"I remember when we didn't have a Quality Assurance department at the hospital. Now we have busybodies carrying around clipboards and issuing citations as if they're speeding tickets. And is our quality better?"

"Why don't you write a letter?"

"I wrote the administration last month when I got called down for doing too many bypasses on Mr. Harlen."

The patient had three narrowings in his arteries and two other less serious obstructions. Heyworth had fixed them all during the operation, yet he'd gotten cited for doing the extra work.

"I can draft a response to this citation pretty quickly," Constance offered.

He shook his head, still looking out at a dense plume of steam billowing up from the hospital's generators. "I'll talk to Drew Shannon about it. Too many people interfering in my practice. It's gone beyond reason."

Constance eased back to the door. "You have a surgery soon," she said to him as he faced away. "You'd better eat your lunch now. I'll get it."

When she left, he put the citation in his pocket and went to work making notes on an index card about his next surgery. Every day, Heyworth ate the same thing at his desk, a routine that kept him focused on larger thoughts. A moment later, she came back, carrying a Tupperware bowl filled with tuna on iceberg lettuce. She placed it on his desk with a glass of water, a plastic fork, and a strip of paper towel.

"You saw the note that Marge called," she said.

Near his elbow, there was a pink slip—it noted only the time of his wife's call, but he knew she'd phoned to remind him of their session that night with the marriage counselor. He nodded at Constance and went on eating his tuna quickly, in big bites, while scribbling notes about the lab findings and X-rays on Mrs. Wilma Ross.

*   *   *

Down on the third floor of the building Heyworth occupied, an enclosed suspension walkway led over to Mercy Hospital. As he passed through the long, tube-like ramp, cars and city buses passed on the avenue beneath him. Through the tinted-glass walls, he saw some of the med center's institutions—a sliver of a tall building, a brick annex linked to a larger structure, the marble facade of a library that faced the broad street.

Except for his internship at a hospital in Boston, an experience so taxing he'd dropped two pounds a day during the first two weeks, Heyworth had spent his career at Mercy Hospital. Founded between the two twentieth-century World Wars, the hospital was built by wealthy philanthropists who gave thousand-dollar bills to ease crises, volunteers who cooked meals in the cafeteria, low-salaried administrators who wanted the opportunity to do meaningful work, and doctors, some of whom were the smartest, most talented of their generation.

Heyworth knew the hospital's history better than that of his own family, and despite all the changes there the past few years, to him it still represented the achievements and the high ideals of medicine.

He was dressed in his scrubs, coat, and shoe covers, his garments swooshing as he walked the hallway. Ahead, Drew Shannon was talking to a nurse.

Heyworth pushed back his sleeve and followed the second hand on his watch as it moved click by click. He needed to get to the operating room. His schedule was tight so he could maximize his billings and keep his long-standing hospital privileges, which included his own operating room. Yet if he could talk to Shannon now, it would save time later.

Shannon's gray-blond hair glistened in the fluorescent light. He wore a neatly pressed white smock with Dept. of Cardiology stitched in blue over his breast pocket.

Shannon was the hospital's medical director, a position more powerful since the unexpected resignation of the Chief Executive Officer five months earlier. For eleven years, Shannon had been a cardiologist at Mercy. Two years ago he'd gotten a degree in medical management at a local university. Now he treated only a few patients each week. Still, this gave him credibility when negotiating with insurance companies and HMOs, and also standing as a practicing physician when he implemented changes at the hospital.

When Shannon looked up, Heyworth caught his eye. "I want to talk to you," he said. "It's about the Quality Assurance cops running around this place."

"You're interrupting a conversation here," Shannon replied. Interactions between the two were never casual, and he hesitated before turning back to the nurse.

Heyworth stepped away and stood beside a gurney. He was not used to waiting; patients, nurses, administrators, typically waited for him. When Shannon finished talking to the young woman, he headed up the hallway.

Heyworth took quick strides after him. "Drew," he said from behind. "Drew!"

Shannon shook his head as if exhausted and turned to Heyworth. "Come," he said, motioning with a nod.

They went into a vacant patient room. Shannon closed the door and adjusted his wire glasses. His eyes were rimmed with red from stress and anxiety. "What is it, Doctor? What now?"

Heyworth held up the yellow citation, letting its bottom dangle.

"I know what a QA form looks like," Shannon said.

Heyworth tapped his forefinger at the bold print on the page. "I got cited here for fluid overload, whatever that means. It's ridiculous."

"You know, other doctors here get QA citations when they're warranted, but they don't fuss about it as much as you do. Nobody fusses about anything here as much as you do."

"I don't like being adversarial," Heyworth said, "but there's a principle involved here."

"What are you talking about?"

"Autonomy. I'm being nibbled to death."

"I realize you think QA is sometimes overzealous."

"Those people don't really produce anything, and with a frivolous citation like this, they sap the energy of those who do."

"David," Shannon said. "The reason we have quality assurance is that our customers want proof we're delivering quality care. There are a lot of pressures out there."

"Talk to me about pressures," Heyworth scoffed. "I've got a seventy-year-old woman waiting for me down in the O.R. right now." He clenched his hand. "She's got an aneurysm in her chest the size of my fist."

"My point," Shannon said, "is that it's not easy managing a hospital these days, and you aren't making it any easier."

Heyworth massaged his temples, looking disgustedly at Shannon. "Drew," he finally said, "you should either practice cardiology, which you used to do quite well, or administer the hospital. One or the other. That just might make your life easier."

"We don't practice medicine in a vacuum. I got involved in administration because I care about the future of this hospital."

"Save the speech, Drew. Remember who you're talking to."

"Forgive me. I'm sorry for caring too much."

"Save the sarcasm too."

Shannon glowered, his broad mouth turned down. "You've never been a team player, have you?"

"Team player," Heyworth repeated. "This hospital was a leader in innovation. Now we have little teams of people, and the Lilliputians are tying the others down."

Shannon shook his head. "The Lilliputians versus the giants. And of course, you're one of the giants. You see medicine that way, don't you? It's an old-fashioned view, Doctor." He started for the door, but Heyworth was in his path and made no effort to move.

"Get out of my way," Shannon said as he brushed past Heyworth. "I was in pretty good spirits until I saw you."

"You never looked into my complaint about my patients getting hustled out of ICU before I think they're ready."

"There wasn't much to that," Shannon said, leaving. "But don't worry, I'll check into this little citation you're so upset about."

*   *   *

Jack Lewis lay flat on the hospital bed, a white sheet stretched from his toes to his chin. His head was half-buried in his pillow, and on his wrinkled, sun-splotched forehead the four stitches from his fall were visible.

His wife, Ann, sat near him in a blue recliner. In her slacks, blouse, and black sneakers, she was dressed for one of her walks around the neighborhood at their new retirement home out in Southpointe, a planned community seventy-five miles east of Madsen. But the only walking she'd done the past two days was up and down the halls of Mercy Hospital. It was the place where the heart doctors in the Lewises' healthcare plan were affiliated.

There were voices outside the doorway. Ann stood when Drew Shannon walked into the room with two nurses trailing him.

"Good morning, Mr. and Mrs. Lewis." Shannon shook Ann's hand measuredly, looking her in the eye, and patted her wrist with his free hand and squeezed her forearm. His grip was warm and soft, and when Ann finally gave him a half-smile, he moved to the bed.

"How you doing there, Mr. Lewis?" he said, his tone upbeat.

Jack's eyes brightened at the doctor's attention.

"The nurse tells me you're still having some chest pain," the doctor went on.

"Yeah, and I've got flat feet and I'm not very pretty either. Did she mention that, too?"

"He's cranky this morning," Ann said.

"No crankier than yesterday. Or the day before," Jack replied. "In fact, I'm not as cranky as you are and I should be the one who's upset about all this."

Shannon turned on the examination light. His long face was expressionless as he pressed the stethoscope to Jack's chest. The doctor knew others at the hospital watched his example in balancing costs and qual-ity in patient care, and after a battery of tests and a period of observa-tion, he'd judged that the blockages in Jack's arteries could be treated with drugs, that they were not life threatening because they seemed to obstruct only thirty percent or so of the arteries' circumference.

Shannon was the only doctor who'd examined Jack Lewis since a pri-mary-care physician first saw him at the hospital out in Southpointe. "You're fortunate to have someone like Dr. Shannon in your network," the physician had told Jack then. Ann had been impressed when she learned Shannon was the medical director at Mercy.

As Ann stood over Jack at the bedside, she looked at the nurses behind her, then at Shannon. "One of the nurses told me you're a pianist," she said, trying to make conversation.

"I play at it," Shannon said, without looking up.

"I tried the harmonica way back when I was in junior high," Jack chimed in. "My sister kept telling me I was crummy, so I quit."

"Okay, Jack," Ann said, annoyed that he'd deflected her talk with the doctor.

Shannon took the prongs of his stethoscope out of his ears. "I'm going to increase your dosage of the anti-anginals, Mr. Lewis. That should help you get back to harmonica playing or whatever else you want to do."

Jack coughed, lifting his head off his pillow. "I intend to get back to playing golf. Sooner the better."

"He plays every weekday, but never on weekends," Ann explained. "Now that he's retired, it's as if golf is his job."

"I'm doing other things with my retirement," Jack said.

"Not many."

"Well, I've got plans. If I ever get out of here."

"I think I asked you where you worked," Shannon said, earnestly try-ing to remember. "You said you were with a funeral-home company, isn't that right?"

"Not just any company." Jack propped his head towards Shannon. "The outfit I worked for ran funeral homes all over the world. You're in health care, right, Doc, well, I was in death care. The death-care business."

"You know by now that he likes to pun and joke," Ann said to Shannon. "He can't help himself."

The doctor turned back to the bed. "Well, as I said, Mr. Lewis, I'm going to increase your dosage of anti-anginals."

"What exactly is the medication supposed to do?" Ann asked.

"It relaxes and opens the arteries."

"Isn't that what we've been trying to do for several days now? It doesn't seem to have helped."

"Remember, the first day at the hospital was for the angiogram, and sometimes the drugs take a little longer. It depends on the patient. Let's give it time." Shannon turned to Jack and touched his shoulder. "You get better now, Mr. Lewis. We're counting on you."

"Thanks, Doctor," Jack said, grinning.

Ann followed Shannon and the nurses out into the hallway. She came up behind him as he made notes on a clipboard.

"Doctor," she said, "My husband's still having trouble breathing at night, and though he didn't tell you about it—I had to pry it out of him myself—he's had jaw pain, too, which is a bad sign. I have a hunch he needs more serious treatment."

"Let's keep on with the medication, Mrs. Lewis." Shannon told her the names of the three drugs he'd prescribed for Jack, trying to reassure her.

Ann looked at the nurses, who seemed ready to move on, and then repeated the name of one of the drugs. "I've seen that advertised in my home-and-garden magazine. It seems like if the drug was very strong, they wouldn't advertise it in there."

"It's not the only medicine we're using." Shannon's face was pale with fatigue, but he smiled at her, full and warm, and touched her arm. "I'll check on your husband a bit later."

Ann watched him walk away. She had little basis for challenging the doctor's diagnosis. She had only a gut feeling, some information about coronary-artery disease she'd gleaned off the Internet, a smattering of dated medical knowledge from six months of nurses' training she had more than thirty-five years ago, before quitting to raise her son, Neal.

Back in the room, Jack faced away from her, his eyes closed. Ann sat in the recliner, and they were both almost asleep when there was a soft knock on the door.

An attendant brought in a plastic tray with a chicken sandwich and a fruit cup. Ann took up a spoon and raised a bite of apple to Jack's mouth as if administering medication.

"I can feed myself, you know," he said as he chewed. "You make me feel like I'm pitiful."

"Please," she said with a sigh, "this makes me feel like I'm doing something to help." She checked to see if the sandwich had mayonnaise on it, and black crumbs fell onto the bedsheet when she lifted the top piece of bread. "It's burnt on bottom," she added as she handed Jack half the sandwich.

Crumbs dropped from his mouth as he ate. Ann moved them off the bed with sharp brushing movements. She thought it clever that the hospital served the bread burnt-side down, knowing it was less noticeable that way.

"This is all pretty crummy, I know," Jack said.

"Don't pun with me anymore." She stroked her hand across the bed to flick off the last dark speck. "Not now. I'm not in the mood for it."

He pulled the sheet up under his chin and his eyes got teary. "Do you love me, hon? In spite of all of this heart-trouble crud?"

"It's not crud, Jack. You're human." Ann kissed his forehead. "Of course I love you. Come on, now."

She spooned up a bite of banana and went on feeding him until he turned sideways into his pillow and nodded off, his arm dangling off the bed's edge. Ann saw the blue-plastic ID band around his wrist and wished they were back home. She could almost smell dinner cooking in her kitchen and see the nook by the back door where Ibi, their Scottish terrier, slept. There were things left undone, she realized: shrubs that needed trimming, boxes to be put away in the attic, the monogrammed silver barrette to be wrapped and mailed for their granddaughter's birthday.

With Jack's retirement, the Lewises had finally moved to Southpointe last winter. It was a planned community with a hometown atmosphere. Residents ranged from those of modest means to the wealthy. Southpointe had a giant mall and a fine-arts pavilion and an affordable golf course that Jack considered the best public course in the region.

Jack's voice jarred Ann from her daydream.

"That light," he said, motioning at the window. "It's right in my eyes."

She went to close the blinds.

"And that cross on the wall there is crooked. Do something with it while you're up."

Ann straightened the ivory cross over Jack's bed, centering the arms of Jesus. "There, how's that?" she said, backing away.

"Still off kilter."

"Well, you're just going to have to put up with it," she said, and then she remembered that during her nurses' training she was told if the patient stopped complaining, it meant he was not noticing his surroundings. "Wait a minute, you're right." She nudged an arm of the cross higher with her thumb. "We can't have a crooked Christ. There. How's that?"

"Better."

She ran her fingers through Jack's thin, silvery hair, careful not to touch his stitches, and as she spread a blanket over him, she smelled a stale odor.

The phone on the bedside table rang, and she hurried to answer it. She stretched the phone cord to get as far away from Jack's bed as possible and cupped the mouthpiece. She spoke softly, bending the truth a little by telling Neal, their son calling from Seattle, that she wasn't overly concerned about Jack's condition. Neal said he was considering coming to Madsen, but she put him off and said she'd call tomorrow when there was more to report.

She lay on her cot. The crossbar pressed into her lower back, and she turned over onto her side, facing the wall. She heard Jack's snoring as she shifted again, trying to get comfortable. She told herself if she were having heart troubles and lying there in that hospital bed, Jack would assert himself to make sure she got the best possible care. She imagined confronting someone and wondered whom she might take on, or if anything would do much good. Her thoughts jumbled, and exhausted, she fell into a shallow sleep.

∗   ∗   ∗

The corridor outside the operating rooms was cluttered with gurneys, tanks of compressed oxygen, cardboard boxes emblazoned with the orange biohazard logo.

Heyworth stood off the hallway at a deep-troughed sink wearing his surgical cap and mask. He spread betadine soap on his hands and forearms with a brush and scrubbed each finger four times on all four planes, and then up his arms, and ran a plastic pick underneath his fingernails. His precise movements mirrored his thoughts: This surgery had to be perfect—Wilma Ross had only one chance at this operation, and she might not recover with anything less than his best.

He put his shoulder into the double-doors and entered the operating room, his wet arms bent up and held out in front of him.

The room smelled of antiseptic and sizzled flesh, blending from the assistant's prep work of opening up the body. Three round lights hovered above the operating table on which the patient lay anesthetized with blue sheets draped over her head and legs.

Heyworth went to one of the nurses. "Hello, Louisa," he said.

"Buenos dias, Doctor." Louisa's brown eyes were magnified by jar-lid glasses, and like the other four attendants in the room, she wore rubber clogs and an operating gown over blue scrubs that looked like pajamas. She handed Heyworth a sterile towel, and he dabbed his arms. Then she offered up his surgical gown, and he put an arm into each sleeve, like a king being dressed, and fitted his hands into the latex gloves she held out at the end of his sleeves.

"Glad you're with me today." He pivoted slightly so she could fasten the button at the back of his neck.

"I don't know if I am," she replied. "You work me too hard."

The two of them had a history: Louisa used to work only in his operating room, but a new hospital policy rotated some nurses with the intention of distributing resources more evenly among doctors. Now, she was paired with him only about one week a month.

"Turn on my music," he said. Heyworth liked classical music when he operated, so he played it even though another new policy discouraged music in the hospital's operating rooms.

"Yes, sir, I was just going to."

"And check the temperature in here while you're at it. It feels too warm for the patient."

As Heyworth walked to the operating table, the anesthesiologist, the perfusionist, and the nurses looked in his direction. The room fell quiet.

"How's it look, Laney?"

Heyworth's surgical assistant was standing over the patient. Before his arrival, she had made an incision from below the patient's shoulder, along the sixth rib, to the navel. The heart was exposed.

"This aneurysm is a doozy," Laney said.

Heyworth looked at the aorta with its thin walls and the swollen, round aneurysm. The bulge was about three inches in diameter. The section of the aorta looked like a garden hose with a golf ball stuffed inside.

"We got to it just in time, if you ask me," Laney said.

Heyworth looked back at the CT scans and X-rays on the wall. He'd seen them before and already decided precisely how much of the aorta needed to be patched to remove the aneurysm. Fixing too little tissue risked a rupture; too much increased the chance of paralysis due to diminished blood flow to the spinal cord during surgery.

"Scalpel," he said to his scrub nurse. She snapped the instrument in his palm, moving with him in a rhythm of anticipation.

He clamped the aorta above the aneurysm and when he cut the aorta, the bleeding began, oozing with each heart beat. Blood was siphoned out, added to, recirculated. Large volumes were required: twenty-one packets of cell savers, twelve packed cells, five units of fresh frozen plasma, two bags of platelets.

Heyworth sliced away the weakened section, dropping chunks of discolored tissue onto a rubber mat across the patient's lower abdomen. Where the bulge in the aorta had been, he inserted an eight-inch length of Dacron tube.

He then restitched the remaining healthy aorta around the tube, moving the curved, tapered needles through the rubbery tissue, favoring neither his left hand nor his right. There was little motion of his arms or shoulders, just his hands moving in a blur, artistic in its efficiency. He stopped stitching only to glance up at the neon-colored lines on the overhead screens that monitored the pulse and body temperature and blood pressure. Heyworth stitched for nearly an hour and when he'd finished setting the graft and the aorta was repaired, the rim of his cap was sweat-stained and the work he'd done looked like a photograph in the medical textbook he'd co-authored on this surgical procedure.

He began closing up the patient, and when Laney could take over, he let her finish. Before he left, he stopped near the metal shelves and looked back into the room, observing the team of surgical staffers he commanded and the heart-lung, anesthesia, and ultrasound machines clustered around the patient. "Great job," he said to himself under his mask. His accomplishments in this operating room had given him more satisfaction than anything else in life. He loved surgery, even considered it fun at times. Yet his frustrations with medicine, brought on by trends that grated against his nature, made moments of triumph like this more difficult to come by.

He stripped off his gloves and gown and went out, passing down the hallway through two sets of double-doors. He asked the nurse behind the high counter in intensive care to page Mr. Ross in the waiting room.

Soon, relatives and friends of Wilma Ross approached him, moving in a solemn single-file march. There were a husband and wife, each carrying a child, three older men in ranchers' caps, several teenagers in T-shirts. A minister in a tie was the last one in, and they all gathered in a semi-circle facing Heyworth.

"Where's Mr. Ross?" he asked into the crowd.

"Here I am." Mr. Ross emerged from the rear. The sleeves of his shirt were rolled high on his weathered biceps, and his wrinkled face was waxen.

"Everything went fine," Heyworth said to him. "Your wife's a real trooper."

Underneath the bill of his cap, Mr. Ross's eyes were moist.

Heyworth gently squeezed his arm. "She came through just fine. No problems. We put the Dacron tube in. Everything was just like I explained yesterday. Your wife is headed to the recovery room. You can see her in a few hours."

The old man's shoulders sagged with relief, with joy. To Heyworth's right, a blond-haired woman asked, "How long will that tube last?"

"Not forever," Heyworth said, grinning. "Only a couple of hundred years."

*   *   *

Heyworth crossed back over the walkway to his office suite. The walls of his reception room, the four inner chambers, even the makeshift kitchen, were decorated with plaques—his bachelor's degree in engineering (with a minor in art history), his medical school diploma, his certificate from the American Board of Thoracic Surgery, a key he'd been presented to the city of Bologna, Italy, his certificate from the International Society for Heart Transplantation and so on.

Low sunlight washed across his desk as he spoke into the speakerphone, dictating his postoperative report.

"An attempt was made to cross clamp the aorta between the left common carotid and left subclavian arteries. However, due to the aberrant recurrent right subclavian aneurysm, it was deemed entirely unsafe and unsuitable to clamp at this level."

Constance came in carrying a file in her hand, but he went on talking robotically: "Consequently, the aorta was clamped distal to the right subclavian artery. The proximal portion of the aneurysm was then opened longitudinally using cautery. End of dictation." He hung up the phone and sighed as his mind changed gears. "That's it for today, Constance. I need to leave early."

She rubbed her chin, puzzled. In the evenings he typically went on rounds to see patients or weaved in another surgery, occasionally staying as late as midnight. "Nothing's wrong, is there?"

"I have to tend to something personal," he said, not mentioning his session with the marriage counselor.

"I guess we can look at the financial statement tomorrow."

He raised an eyebrow. "You have it prepared already?"

She handed him the papers inside the file she held, and as he flipped through them, his eyes went to the bottom line, like any entrepreneur.

"How can I work harder and harder and earn less and less money?"

"Managed care."

"That was a rhetorical question, Constance." Heyworth's brow tensed as he studied the pages. It frustrated him when he thought of how much he paid for malpractice insurance—some months it was almost half his costs—and after he reconciled himself to this, he focused on the top line. "I don't know what the administration is doing with my billings, and they don't either. I should never have let them take over my billing in the first place."

"You didn't have a choice," she said, and then added hopefully, "Think they'll let you get it back?"

He shook his head. "They're also deducting more each month as my so-called contribution to the surgery department." It was futile to talk about it. "What's the schedule for tomorrow?"

"You have a bypass first thing, Mrs. Rosenbaum, and then a thoraco at two-thirty on that young man, Mr. Markle. If you want to go really late, Mrs. Koshmarian is a possibility. It looks like the usual jam-packed day." As she stood over him, Constance glanced at the wall clock. "I have to go myself in a few minutes. I have to pick up my son today."

Heyworth looked up.

"He's in a new program for children with Down's syndrome. I have a hunch this won't work out either, but my husband's keen on trying it."

"Your intuition is eerily accurate on most things. But I hope it goes well. Do you need time off to get him settled in the program?"

"Not now. It's okay."

Heyworth looked back down at the financial statement, cupping his eyes. "Are you sure this number is right? I could swear I billed more than this last month."

"Medicare cut the payment rates for surgical procedures."

"I thought they already did that last year."

"Yes, sir, they did. But they've pared it back more."

He pondered the numbers on the page, then thought of charity work he'd done that wasn't accounted for, and went on: "How much work have we written off this year as uncollectible?"

"It's not on the financial statement, but there's a lot more to be written off. I'd say around a hundred and fifty thousand dollars or so."

"What do you mean 'around'?"

"I'll get the exact number." She worked hard to anticipate his demands because he liked to be precise. "Just a minute."

"Hold it," he said, taking off his smock. "You need to go, and so do I. I'll be here in the morning at seven o'clock."

CHAPTER 2

Heyworth drove his Mercedes sedan along the outskirts of the medical complex. The sun was setting through the brume of humidity over the city. He passed a church with a marquee advertising aerobics classes, a row of large houses built on tiny lots where small homes once stood.

From the freeway, he turned off into Morningside, an old-money neighborhood or as old as money could be in a Sunbelt city like Madsen. Heyworth's house, on a big corner lot, was like a small chateau, with coarse stone finish and a slate mansard roof. The driveway ran between two massive oak trees.

He parked beside his daughter's teal-colored sports car. The buzz of crickets and katydids greeted him when he got out. At the back door, he petted Cab, the golden retriever he'd named for the acronym for cardiovascular artery bypass.

Marge Heyworth stood at the sink, chopping celery. Her lemondrop earrings jangled and her brown hair was pinned back, framing her elegant, lightly freckled face. She had always lived well; her father, who'd died in a small-plane crash ten years ago, was a modestly successful merchant. Yet she had an unconventionality expressed by the quirky bracelets she sometimes wore, the rings on her middle-and forefingers (even into her middle forties, she'd worn matching rings on her second toes), the clothes that were sometimes avant-garde for the Morningside neighborhood.

"How are you?" Heyworth said. He kissed the back of her neck, and her shoulder muscles pinched together as she held her hands underneath the faucet. She'd spent the last half-hour wondering if another emergency or sick patient would again take over his evening and crowd out their counseling session.

"Get out of those scrubs," she said, glancing back. "Hurry now."

Heyworth went back to the bedroom and changed, slipping on the drawstring pants that Marge had gotten for him on Elizabeth Street during one of her shopping trips to New York and an orange-red Hawaiian shirt he'd bought, one of the few carefree garments in his closet. The tropical motif seemed appropriate to him, given the mid-August heat.

When Heyworth came back into the kitchen, Marge was arranging asparagus spears in crisscrosses on the plate. "I'm making us a sandwich and a salad." She swallowed the last drops from her wine glass as she turned to him. "You look like Don Ho in that shirt."

The kitchen door swung open and their daughter Aline came in. She wore gray DKNY sweats and had just showered after hitting tennis balls with her instructor at the racquet club. She ranked among the city's top eighteen-year-old players.

"You fed Cab yet?" Heyworth asked.

"No," Aline said. Her face was very tan and there was a striking symmetry to her eyes and lips and cheekbones.

"You're about to go off to college, and you're feeling above chores like feeding a poor dog," he said.

Aline pulled back her frizzy hair as she opened the refrigerator, and Heyworth noted with dismay the silver ring threaded through the edge of her left eyebrow. Last fall, during one of her tennis matches, he'd been shocked to see the starburst tattoo on her back just below her neckline. Even Marge had been startled by the New Age tattoo's indelible permanence.

"Doesn't that hurt to get those piercings done around your eyes?"

"David," Marge said. "Be serious now. You cut people open every day in surgery, even if they are anesthetized."

"Friends of mine have pierced their tongues, even their chins." Aline flashed her blue eyes at Heyworth to gauge his reaction. "One girl has a chain from the spike in her nostril over to her earring. The chain just dangles across her face. This other guy, Jimmy Hays—you know him, Mom—he has spikes in his skull, a tongue stud, and another right there." She touched a spot above the cleft in her chin.

Heyworth winced. "You're too smart to do something like that, Aline."

Marge put two plates on the island in the middle of the kitchen. "Getting a piercing is a rite of passage for these high school kids. We all experiment and do some crazy things. I know I did. Pull up a stool, Aline. We're going to eat at the counter tonight."

"I'm taking mine upstairs," she said as she picked up her dish. "I'm downloading some music on the Internet, and besides I need to start packing."

"Your father and I are going out," Marge said.

Aline walked on, nibbling on an asparagus spear. "Lock the back door when you leave, please. Thank you."

"We'll be back in an hour and a half or so, and I'll help you pack then."

"I've got it under control," Aline said, walking out.

"So you don't need me."

"Just not right now, Mom. I'm doing pretty good with all of it."

Heyworth watched Aline leave. He occasionally ate dinner with her. Most days, he saw her only a few minutes at a time, though longer on his Saturday afternoons off or on Sunday mornings before he went to the hospital. He'd been unable to attend her dance recitals, school meetings, most of her tennis matches. The spouses of doctors usually understand such trade-offs, but children never do.

He looked at Marge as he heard Aline go upstairs. "I wish she would eat with us. I don't see much of her."

"That's not her fault."

"I'm not saying it's her fault, Marge." He bit into his sandwich. "Does she know we're seeing a marriage counselor?"

"I tell her everything because she finds out anyway. It amazes me sometimes the things she knows."

"And some of the things she wants these days, too."

They'd had discussions about Aline's tastes. She'd always had her own mind about such matters, particularly clothes. The last few years Aline's wardrobe had run towards the trendy and expensive. Heyworth and Marge had argued over whether her sensibilities bordered on the tarty.

"You're still mad because she doesn't have a job this summer," Marge said. "But she's working hard on her tennis. She doesn't have as much natural ability as some of the other girls."

"She needs to show some appreciation for how money is earned."

"You gave me that speech last summer right after she told you she didn't want to work in your office. Sometimes I wonder if you even know her."

They finished eating and then drove in Marge's silver BMW to a midtown neighborhood full of bed-and-breakfasts and historic homes with latticed woodwork.

The marriage counselor's office was on the top floor of an olive-colored Victorian house. Heyworth felt awkward as he met Vanessa Stoy, but Marge was more at ease because she'd seen Vanessa twice by herself in the last month.

Vanessa was Marge's age, four years younger than Heyworth. She had red hair, and her loose-fitting, blousey pants flowed behind her as she moved across the hardwood floor. She sat in a wicker-backed chair while Heyworth and Marge settled down at opposite ends of a worn corduroy couch.

The soft light of a late-summer evening filtered through the wooden shutters. It had been a dry summer, but outside the sky had quickly filled with dark clouds.

Heyworth reached for a glass of water on the low table. "Marge told me a little bit about you."

"You're curious about my credentials. Most of my doctor clients ask about that," Vanessa replied. "I don't have a medical degree, and I'm not a psychiatrist. I'm a licensed social worker, and I have fifteen years experience working with couples, many of them with one or both spouses in medicine."

Heyworth sank into the sofa. Because Marge had sought out Vanessa—she was recommended by her friend Colette—he still wondered if she could view their marriage objectively.

"Tell me how you two are doing?" Vanessa said.

Heyworth and Marge stared ahead, hands on their knees, like children in for a scolding.

"One of you is going to have to speak first," Vanessa said. "It's unavoidable."

"We're not happy in our marriage now," Marge said. "At least I'm not."

Vanessa focused on Marge, as if Heyworth weren't there. "You used the word, 'now.' When *were* you happy in the marriage?"

"In the early years, it seemed like we were."

"We've been happy more than that," Heyworth said.

"Okay," Vanessa said, turning to him. "There are no right and wrong answers here. There are only feelings and feelings are neither right or wrong." She folded her feet under her yoga-style and sat higher. "Are you happy now in the marriage, David?"

"If I didn't think things could be better, I wouldn't have agreed to come see you."

Vanessa studied Heyworth, who had his arms crossed, and then she turned back to Marge. "How were things different when you were happy?"

"We were younger, of course, and building a family and struggling together and working towards a common purpose." Marge looked down and then quickly up at Vanessa as her memory stirred. "Really, though, as I've thought back on our marriage, I've realized David's never had time for our relationship. During our early years, he'd come home late from the hospital and then go out to do his running. We went to Florida just before we had Aline—that was the first real vacation we'd had together in years. And now as we get older, it seems we should have more time for each other, but we don't. He even works Christmas Day. The Hagers, my friends from down at the theater, have gone camping together on the beaches in Costa Rica."

"Marge has gone with me on several trips—to northern Italy, to Belgium," Heyworth explained. "I speak at conferences overseas. And Hawaii. She and I went there. That's where I got this shirt."

"Those trips are work for you, David. It's not the same thing."

He stared at the coffee table, at the pen resting on a ceramic platter.

"How do you feel about what Marge is saying?" Vanessa asked.

"I've worked very hard the past several years, I admit."

"You've had one week of pure vacation in the last four years, David," Marge said. "One week."

"Why have you worked so hard?" Vanessa asked.

"Why?" he repeated. "Well, I love my work. That's always been true." He looked at his hands, clasped tightly in his lap. "I guess I fear the future of medicine and my place in it so much so that I've felt compelled to work harder than ever. There's a lot of change in my practice, and it makes me anxious. I've dealt with it by trying to get ahead professionally and financially while it's still possible."

"How does this fit in with your marriage?" Vanessa asked.

"Marge likes the good things my work brings—her freedom to do charity work or work at the theater, our house that she's decorated so beautifully, our daughter's private schooling, the standing in the community. This hasn't been all just for me...." His voice trailed off.

Beside him, Marge clutched a small pillow to her chest. "For years I told myself the best place for David was in the operating room," she said. "That was what he was good at. It was where he belonged. He was helping people, I rationalized. So I took the philosophy that I'd take the hours I had and use them to better the community. I poured myself into activities—fund-raisers, causes for disadvantaged children, the theater over the past few years. I've done some interior decorating for friends who asked me. I haven't done anything very serious with my artistic talent, though."

"I think one reason Marge is having a hard time is because our daughter, Aline, is going away to college early next week."

"David, you can't simplify our problems like that," Marge said sharply, then turned to Vanessa. "I admit Aline's leaving upsets me. She's become my best friend, really."

"You put a lot into raising her?"

"I had to give a lot. I didn't have a lot of help."

Before Aline was conceived, Heyworth had tried to convince Marge not to have a baby, saying he was so consumed by his medical practice that it wouldn't be fair to Marge or to the child. They never discussed it again after Aline was born.

There was a grumble of thunder, and the tree limbs rustled against the lattice on the side of the house.

Heyworth leaned forward. "Marge and I have talked some about our marriage. Over the last few months, I've made it a point to be home early at least one night a week so we could spend more time together."

As he spoke, Vanessa scribbled on a notepad. Then she said, "Do you two want to be together?"

They both sat back. In the quiet, the rain came down in heavy drops on the window ledges.

"You're speaking of divorce?" Marge said. She leaned forward abruptly and put her hands over her eyes.

"Tell us what you feel," Vanessa said.

"Relief," Marge said through her fingers. "I've worried for years about keeping our marriage together."

Heyworth watched as she began sniffling. "I think we should've sought help sooner," he said to Vanessa. "That's what I think."

"That's what you think," Vanessa said. "Tell us what you feel."

"I'm just numb right now," he said.

"You live a lot of your life in your head, don't you?"

"What do you mean?"

"You're very serious."

"People have told me that all my life, even my father because I have my mother's temperament. Yet whenever someone says I'm too serious, I have a hard time understanding what they're talking about."

"Then tell me how you feel, and I'll quit talking about it."

"All right." The vein running up his forehead swelled. "I feel scared, damned scared. Professionally, it seems like I'm losing control. My ability to make my own decisions is being eroded by a number of outside forces, and I'm affected by Aline's leaving too, and to add to all this the idea of losing Marge—" He looked away into a corner of the room.

"You were about to say something more," Vanessa said.

"Nothing," and then he added, "I was going to elaborate on my frustrations with my work."

"Does Marge know about these frustrations?"

"I don't discuss them much with her. There are important facets of my life that she doesn't really know about anymore. "

"Is that true, Marge?" Vanessa asked.

"David has a lot of anger in him. It surfaces at inopportune moments. It's painful to converse with him sometimes. You don't know what he's going to get upset about, or go off on."

"Can you give us an example?" Vanessa said.

Marge sat up straighter. "The Hagers, my friends from the theater I was telling you about. They came over for dinner one Saturday night, and we were having a nice conversation out on the patio, mostly about their travels and the theater and some movies we'd seen. We were having a wonderful time when the conversation somehow turned and David suddenly got into an argument with Milt about health care. It got so heated that I was embarrassed."

"I'm not going to have my values attacked in my own home."

"You weren't attacked, David! Don't exaggerate."

Vanessa held up her hand to referee and then looked at Marge. "It sounds like you're angry about David's anger."

"I'm mostly frustrated."

"How so?"

"I don't know," she said. "I guess, I—"

"Go on," Vanessa said. "To make progress, you have to be honest."

"I've found myself interested in other men. This scares me."

There was the sound of rain blowing hard against the windows. Heyworth leaned back into the couch. Marge had never spoken romantically of another man to him, and there was a queasy, sickening flutter in his gut.

"Go on," Vanessa said.

"I met a man at the theater. His name is Sid." Marge rocked back and forth as she talked on: "He works in stage direction and he's also a painter. I've always wanted to pursue my painting seriously—I named my daughter after Gauguin's daughter, for goodness sake—and I've gotten involved at the theater so I could be around more artistic people, though I'm in fund-raising of all things. Anyway, that's why I've become close to the Hagers and that's why Sid and I are—"

"Are what?" Vanessa asked.

"We eat lunch together once a week. We've gone shopping together a time or two. He let me work on the sets he was designing for that Chekhov play, *The Cherry Orchard*."

"You're fond of him?" Vanessa said.

"Of Sid? I thought so." Marge clutched the pillow again. "He and I were on our way to lunch last week, leaving downtown. It was a gorgeous day, not too hot, and he asked if I wanted to see his apartment. He lives in a small studio—lots of canvases and a cramped feeling to it. We drank some wine, not a good idea for me at lunch." She bit her lip. "He tried to kiss me. I stopped him because it didn't feel right. It was very awkward. I shouldn't have gone to his place."

Heyworth saw Vanessa look at him. He stared down, his eyes intense like when he was in his operating room trying to will something to happen. Yet he realized he could not affect what was unfolding. He wanted to get up and leave.

"Then what happened?" Vanessa asked Marge.

"We went back to the theater, and I went on making my fund-raising calls. That's all."

"How did all that make you feel?"

"In some ways, it felt nice to be wanted." Her voice was empty and a little sad.

Heyworth got up and paced behind the couch, running his fingers through his gray-black hair. "Is that all that happened between you two?"

"I told you I didn't feel right about it, David. I haven't been to lunch or anything with him since."

"Why don't you sit down, David," Vanessa said.

"Not now. Just a minute." His footsteps echoed on the hard floor and after a few more turns, he stepped in front of the couch. Marge turned sideways toward him.

"You spend all day at the hospital," she said. "I don't really know what you do with your time or who you see. Hospitals are notorious for breeding romances."

"I have no secrets. You can be sure of that."

"I don't either. I've told you everything."

The two of them sat back on the couch. The rain had stopped, and a grandfather clock ticked away in the stillness.

"Tell me how you feel right now," Vanessa said to Heyworth.

"You heard the tone of my voice."

He got up again and went to the bay windows. The sky had cleared to the west, and the sun was setting under a cap of purple clouds. Marge said "Excuse me" and went to the bathroom. Heyworth stood with his back to Vanessa, and finally she told him she was going to make tea as she also went downstairs.

Heyworth stared at the tops of the houses up the road and indignation thickened his throat. He wondered how Marge could carry on a dalliance with another man. Yet he'd contributed to her feelings, he knew, because for over twenty years he'd thought he could be married to both his wife and his work.

There were footsteps on the stairs. Marge came and stood beside him and put her arm loosely around his midsection.

"I'm going to walk around the neighborhood for a little while," he said, pulling away. "Don't wait. I'll call a taxi when I'm ready to come home."

"You sure?" she said, sounding spent. She lingered, but he had nothing else to say.

He went downstairs a few minutes later and stood out on the porch as Marge was driving off. After he said goodbye to Vanessa, he walked across the street.

The road was wet, and a trace of the sky reflected off the glass storefronts. He peered in the antique shops and then eyed a place that sold handmade furniture. He had never been inside these stores, had never even noticed them before. The thought flashed in his head that there were worlds near him he never encountered, and for the first time in years the sensation that life was passing him by washed over him. And then he wondered: What you've done has been worth it, hasn't it? You made the right choices, didn't you? Ten years ago you could say that it was worth it. Doubts didn't exist. And five years ago, it probably still was. But is it, now? he thought. He walked on and finally stopped at a cafe.

When the taxi took him home, it was almost ten o'clock. The lights burning at his house swelled out into the darkness, and the grass along the driveway was soggy from the rain and from the sprinkler system that went off at preset intervals.

Heyworth went back to the bedroom and saw Marge under the covers. She typically responded to stressful situations by shutting her system down, going to sleep.

Back in the kitchen, Aline was stooped over Cab, holding one of his paws. "What's up, doggy-dog? What's up?" Cab howled and Aline turned up her chin and howled with him.

"You two pipe down," Heyworth said. "Your mother's asleep."

Aline quit petting Cab and started for the door. "I'm going back upstairs. I'm tired, too."

"Let's watch some TV," he said, his tone inviting. "Come sit with me for a minute."

"You know I hate financial news."

"We'll watch whatever you want to watch. Come on. For just a minute."

He went to his chair, and Aline sat on the ottoman. She picked up the remote control and whisked through the channels.

"You get much packing done?" he said as he watched over her shoulder.

"Yes. But I've got too much stuff. I can tell that already."

"You think you're going to have fun at the university?"

"Mom says I can come home and go to Madsen College if I don't like it," Aline said, still facing the TV. "It's my safety school, I guess."

Heyworth had tried to set Aline's sights on an Ivy League school, but her grades and test scores were not quite high enough. At Marge's urging, she'd gotten an application for the Rhode Island School of Design. He wanted her to go to Williams College in Massachusetts, where she'd been accepted, and taper off her tennis, but Aline thought the small college town seemed dull and instead she decided to go to the big state university and try to earn a spot on the tennis team as a walk-on.

Heyworth went around the corner to the foyer to turn off the front lights. There, he saw fragments of a crystal vase shattered on the floor and on the nap of the oriental rug.

"What happened?" Aline said, entering.

Heyworth was bent down over the broken glass as the dog ambled in. "Hold him. He'll cut his paws."

"Maybe the maid broke it."

"Maybe. Or maybe Cab knocked it over earlier today."

He put the larger shards of glass into a pile while Aline herded the dog into the kitchen. He thought it possible that Marge had broken the vase in frustration when she'd arrived home from Vanessa Stoy's office. But someone could have brushed it off the table on entering the house. He checked the front door to make sure it was locked.

"Did you hear anything earlier?" he asked when Aline came back from the kitchen.

"No," she said, frowning. Though their home was in one of the safest neighborhoods in the city, she, like Marge, sometimes became fixated on the idea of somebody breaking into the house. "Do you think someone tried to rob us?"

"No," he said. "But let's check around."

They walked through the first floor—the living room, the ten-chair dining room, the den, the game room, the two guest bedrooms—turning on lights, looking in. They went out on the flagstone patio, staring at the swimming pool, the pin lights in the trees shining down on Marge's rosebushes, the shadows of leaves on the thick grass. The motion sensor wasn't on. Nothing looked suspicious. They checked the patio doors and the French doors off the master bedroom to make sure they were locked.

Then Aline asked him to come upstairs and look around.

In her bedroom suite, there were magazines and books on her bed, loose CDs, empty soda cans, a new Apple computer. Black jeans, tennis skirts, platform shoes were strewn on the floor of her large walk-in closet.

She grinned mischievously as she stood over the open suitcase. "I'll clean this place up a little tomorrow."

Heyworth thought how in a week, Aline's closet would be emptied of most of her possessions. "You keep your room how you want."

"I probably shouldn't have asked you to come up here."

"It's okay," he said. "I'm glad you did."

She walked ahead of him down the stairs to the foyer, where she held the dustpan while he swept the broken glass into a pile. He picked with his fingertips at the small flecks left in the floor's grooves.

"Let me do that," Aline said, bending down. "You won't be able to do surgery if you cut yourself." She blew along the length of the floor boards, dislodging the tiny flecks of glass, and when she finished, she gave him a quick kiss on the cheek. "Sleep tight, Daddy."

She mounted the stairs, taking two steps with each stride, and Heyworth heard her bedroom door shut. Such moments had not passed often between them, he realized, and the ease with which this had happened made him wonder how much he'd missed out on over the years.

He went to his study and got out his leather diary. Every day he made notes in it: his meaningful interactions at work, jottings about the affairs of his office, any subtle improvements or innovations in the techniques he'd used in surgery.

He thought of what had unfolded earlier at Vanessa Stoy's house. He'd always assumed Marge was there for him and knowing he could no longer take this for granted jarred him. He put his diary away.

He went to the back of the house, and as he walked by habit to his side of the bed, he stopped. He didn't feel right sleeping with Marge tonight, he realized. He whispered to her that he was going to the guest bedroom, but she was groggy and barely responded.

Down the hallway, he turned on a bedside lamp, one Marge had bought decades ago for the den in their first house. The sheets were stiff, the pillow too soft. He tossed around in the bed and wondered: What would his life be like if he gave up medicine? How would it affect him? His family?

In the morning, Marge was up before he'd gotten up to take his customary morning run on a hill not too far from the house. She stood in the doorway of the guest bedroom, dressed in a turquoise Japanese kimono and brown slippers.

"Hello," she said to him as he looked at her out of one eye. "Don't hold last night against me."

"I found a broken vase in the foyer last night. Someone must have knocked it off."

"Maybe it was Frank," she said, referring to the handyman who did household upkeep and repairs for them that Heyworth had neither the time nor the aptitude for. "He's been in and out of the front door this week while working on the air conditioner."

"I guess."

Marge turned towards the kitchen. "When Aline leaves next week, I need to—" She sighed and looked back at him. "What I'm trying to say is that I've been thinking of taking a trip, to the Himalayas, the Andes, or the Amazon, somewhere that would stretch me and get me out of the rut I feel like I'm in."

Recently, she'd bought several issues of an outdoor-adventure magazine. She'd also commented to Heyworth a few months ago that she felt as if she were using only ten or twenty percent of herself, at most, and then she'd added that she wanted to "live harder."

"Do you think a trip like that is a good idea right now?"

She shrugged. "Can you clear your schedule tonight? I know this makes two nights in a row, but we can talk some more if you want to."

"I'll try to be home early," he said.

CHAPTER 3

Ann Lewis walked down the second floor of Mercy Hospital, past offices flagged with a metal placard above each doorway—Procurement, Quality Assurance, Ethics and Compliance, Medical Records.

She stepped into the office near the corridor's end marked Patient Representative. No one was there, and she considered coming back later because it was still only a few minutes before nine o'clock in the morning.

On her way out, she looked inside an adjoining office, where a man sat facing a computer. He was obviously busy, but she went in anyway. She told him she wanted to see somebody about her husband's treatment and he said someone in the Patient Representative's office would be in soon.

Ann saw the nameplate on his desk as she came closer. The man's hair was silvery-gray, his eyebrows and mustache dark black. "Mr. Probert," she said, "my husband, Jack Lewis, is in Room 2317. He's been in the hospital several days now if anybody up here wants to know."

Probert didn't know what to do with her. He'd come in early to review some programming without interruption. "Do you know your husband's ID number?"

"I can barely remember my own Social Security number. But his name is Jack Lewis. I told you that a minute ago."

Probert tapped in Jack's name on his keyboard to pull up his medical records.

"My husband's rather fluey," Ann said, "and he's no better this morning though Dr. Shannon, his doctor, apparently thinks he's doing okay. That's what he said yesterday."

"Well, ma'am," Probert said, looking up suddenly, "Dr. Shannon is one of our finest cardiologists."

"I still want to get a second opinion." She sat on an arm of a chair. "Something's not right about my husband's treatment. I feel like I'm getting the runaround."

Probert rubbed his dark brow and put his hand thoughtfully to his mouth. "I'll tell you what, Mrs. Lewis. If it'll make you feel better, I'll make sure someone on our staff checks it out."

Ann repeated Jack's room number, and Probert assured her he'd get her story to the right people. She started to say "thank you" but didn't want to seem too grateful.

She left his office, walking head down toward the elevator when up ahead, a door slammed. The sharp crack lured a heavyset clerical worker from a nearby office out into the hallway. Ann met the woman where the door had shut, and the two of them peered like voyeurs through a narrow window. Inside, two men stood eye to eye, their arms waving, their heads bobbing in anger. One man wore a business suit and the other a doctor's white coat. Ann tried to hear what the men were saying, but their voices were faint through the windowpane, and then they were drowned out by the heavyset woman's talking: "That Dr. Heyworth," she said to Ann. "People come from all over to get their hearts fixed by that man, but he's just the most hard-headed doctor around here. He's always taking on somebody or something, it seems."

Ann went on looking inside the office while the woman walked away. Then as Heyworth came towards the closed door, she heard his voice more clearly:"Don't hurry my patients out. I'll decide when they are to be released. I'm telling you one last time."

Ann walked to the elevator. Up on the third floor, she covered exactly two tiles with each step because she considered it a bad omen to get off stride. In the distance, down the corridor toward Jack's room, she saw Dr. Shannon's angular silhouette. She stopped abruptly, her shoes squeaking on the floor. A knot of people in white coats and blue scrubs gathered around Shannon. Then, after a brief consultation, he pushed through the huddle and started up the hallway with two doctors alongside.

Ann didn't want to talk to him, so she stepped into an alcove and hid, covered to her waist by a red crash cart used for hospital emergencies. Before Shannon reached the alcove, he turned off and went down another corridor, but the two young doctors he'd been walking with continued up the main hallway. Ann heard one of them speak:

"There's always a gray area of judgment. I think there was enough to justify it. I hated to do it, but I had to reverse the diagnosis."

The other voice was gruff. "We just need to move on. Her condition is not worth spending much more on."

Ann came out of the alcove after they passed and walked briskly down to Jack's room.

Jack said "hey" weakly when she came in. His bed faced away from her, and she leaned back against the door, smoothing her blouse, trying to slow her breathing.

Finally, she stepped to the bed. "Was Dr. Shannon just by here?"

He shook his head as he watched the TV high on the wall.

"Jack! I asked you a question."

He looked sharply at her. "No, he wasn't. Do I have to spell it out? What's gotten into you, anyway?"

As he turned back to the TV, Ann picked up the phone on the bed-side table to call her son, Neal. But then she realized she couldn't speak candidly in front of Jack.

"Who you calling?" Jack asked right before she hung up.

"Neal's not home tonight. I just remembered."

"Where is he?"

"How're you feeling?" she said, trying to change the subject.

"Pretty much the same as the last time you asked me."

She sat in the recliner. She often consulted God for guidance, for reaffirmation of her gut feelings and instincts. She got her Bible out of her oversized purse and opened it at random to Proverbs and read several paragraphs. She closed her eyes. The only sound in the room was a thin tinny squawk coming from the pillow speaker beside Jack's head. Moments later, Jack knocked an empty Coke can off the bedside table. She put a bookmark in her Bible and picked up the can.

"Sorry," Jack said, looking sideways at her. "At least the thing was empty."

Ann saw his hand shaking slightly. "Are you all right?"

Jack nodded "yes" weakly.

She turned to the azalea plant on the windowsill and poked her fingertip into its soil. "It's so dry in here," she said, gazing out at the sharp light on the opposite wing of the hospital. "But I'll bet it's almost a hundred degrees outside and humid, too."

In the small bathroom, she drew a cup of water and gazed into the mirror. Her hair was matted in clumps, the gray roots exposed. She brushed it and put on lipstick and rouge and then went out toward the door, careful not to let Jack see her freshly made-up face.

He heard her footsteps. "Why don't you just sit here beside me awhile?"

"I'm just going to run a little errand," she said. "I'll be back before your next TV show comes on."

*　　　*　　　*

Down in the lobby, ficus trees reached for the sunlight in the high ceiling. Near the front entrance, a columnar directory listed the hospital's doctors. Ann noted Heyworth's office number and crossed the walkway to his building.

The heavy door to his waiting room closed behind her like a vault. At the far end a sign read: "Please ring bell and be seated."

Ann pressed the buzzer three times. When the pane slid open a young woman, a secretary who reported to Constance, asked if she had an appointment. Ann said no, but that she would wait to see Dr. Heyworth anyway. She took some forms from the receptionist and filled them out with Jack's medical history and handed it all back.

After this, for lack of anything else to do, Ann read one of the plaques above the couch, then another. These credentials and training certificates and licensures on the walls revealed Heyworth's background and depth of expertise. She stepped from one plaque to the next, moving around the room, and when she finished, she told herself she felt better. But after she sat on the couch, she thought: Don't get too comfortable because you don't really have anything yet.

She looked through the opaque window over the counter to the doctor's office, but behind it there were only fuzzy shadows. There was a large-type Readers' Digeston the coffee table. She read four articles. Forty-five minutes passed. She nodded off, then woke up and realized she'd been away from Jack for almost an hour and a half.

At the far end of the waiting room, the door opened, and there was the solid clank of its closing. Heyworth, just out of surgery, came in. He stopped at the armoire and took out a freshly laundered white smock from among several hanging on a rod.

Ann met him as he turned. "Doctor," she said, her voice throaty.

"Hi there."

She spoke louder, but tried not to seem desperate. "Doctor, my name is Ann Lewis. I'm not a patient of yours, but if you have time—"

"Give me just a minute, Mrs. Lewis."

Heyworth slung his smock over his shoulder and went past her, into the interior of his office suite.

*   *   *

On Heyworth's desk, there was a pile of message slips: a reminder about next week's mortality and morbidity conference, a query about the status of a patient in post-op, a call from a young doctor he'd met in Italy last year who wanted to come train with him.

Constance came in. "How'd surgery go?" she asked, curious about the bypass operation on Mrs. Rosenbaum.

"Pretty much perfect," he said. "Almost." He propped his feet up— he'd been on them for three hours in surgery. "What's the story on the woman in the waiting room?"

"You saw her?" Constance said, as if offended.

"My smock's dirty." Heyworth pointed to bloodstains on one sleeve. "I had to get a new one out of the closet, so I came in through the main door instead of the back way."

Constance wrinkled her nose. She took it as a personal failure if he had to perform ordinary office chores she'd failed to anticipate. "I'd have gotten that for you."

"Never mind my smock. What about the woman out there?"

"Before I forget, your wife called. Marge made me promise to have you call her. You can do it while I get the forms the lady filled out from the front desk."

Heyworth phoned Marge at the theater, but she had just gone to an early lunch.

When he hung up, Constance came back and handed him some papers on a clipboard. "This Mrs. Lewis seems determined to see you today. The receptionist told me she's been waiting awhile."

"Go get her. I've got a few minutes."

Heyworth emptied the pockets of his dirty smock, stripped it off, and put on the fresh one. It was pressed stiff, and when he pushed his arm into the sleeve, the starch ripped.

Moments later, Constance stood at the door and ushered Ann into the office.

Ann's eyes scanned the tall bookcases behind Heyworth, the stacks of patient files on his large desk. "I know you're busy, Doctor," she said as she gripped the top of the chair across from him.

"Please. Have a seat, Mrs. Lewis."

"I'll try to get to the point, here," Ann said as she situated herself. "I saw you this morning down on the second floor."

"You did?" he said, thinking that he did not remember seeing her.

"My husband came to the hospital two days ago for heart problems. He's pale and clammy, and his blood pressure is weak, and he has chest pains and breathes awfully heavy at times, it seems to me, and he has an ache in his jaw occasionally which is a sign of poor circulation." She sat back in her seat. "He's being treated with drugs, but he doesn't seem better. I want a second opinion. From somebody knowledgeable."

"I'm happy to talk to you, Mrs. Lewis." Heyworth glanced at the forms she'd filled out and saw Shannon was the cardiologist on the case. He tried not to let his expression show he was nonplussed. "What does your husband's doctor say?"

"He's basically telling us that some medication and better health habits will take care of it. To tell you the truth, he hasn't been very forthright in answering my questions."

"What have you asked him?"

"Oh, you know. When my husband will be better. Or if he needs more serious treatment. Things like that."

Heyworth looked at her, his lips tight as he swallowed.

"I guess I could have thought of better questions," Ann added. "I don't know."

"Those sound like good ones to me."

Ann leaned toward the doctor's desk. "I talked to the administration about a second opinion this morning. I told a Mr. Probert over there that I had a feeling something wasn't right. He told me he'd have somebody check into my husband's case. I've seen him really go downhill in the past year."

Ann wiped her eyes with the flat of two fingernails. Heyworth handed her a tissue.

"He says he's not in pain," she went on, "but he hasn't been himself, and besides I know he has been in pain. I guess he's like most men in that he doesn't like to admit how he feels, or even that he's sick at all."

"I see." Heyworth had encountered many cases where spouses had disagreements about the nature and seriousness of the problem.

"Do you think you can do anything for him, Doctor?"

Heyworth rocked back in his swivel chair. Jack Lewis wasn't his patient; there'd been no referral from Shannon, no effort to involve him or any other doctor in the case. "I could discuss your husband's case with Dr. Shannon," he said.

Ann frowned at the reluctance in Heyworth's voice. "Will that help, do you think?"

"Perhaps. But I'm not sure." Heyworth crossed his arms. He knew Shannon would not appreciate him meddling.

"Doctor, there's something else I should tell you." She moved up to the edge of her seat. "It's just that I don't think I can trust Dr. Shannon, and since he's the medical director here, I'm worried I can't trust any other doctors here either. I hope you don't take that wrong."

Heyworth pinched his nose and gazed out at the clear sky beyond his big window. Before he could question Ann further, she spoke: "I really should talk to someone else in the Patient Representative's office, but that Mr. Probert was the only person I could find around there early this morning. He was somebody to talk to, I guess." She lowered her head. "I'm sorry I've bothered you—"

There was a sudden, sharp pounding on the wall opposite Heyworth. Both of them looked there until it stopped. Then another burst of thuds shook the wall.

"Excuse me a moment," Heyworth said, rising.

He went out into the hall to the nook where X-rays and CT scans were stored. Constance stood there holding a hammer in one hand and in her other a framed placard, one of Heyworth's updated training certificates.

"Can't that wait?" he said.

As if to justify her interruption, she turned around the plaque to show him the front of it. "I figured you wanted it mounted sooner rather than later."

"I'm trying to have a conversation in my office right now."

"I'm sorry. The nail's already in the wall. I'm done."

Constance glanced over Heyworth's shoulder, and when he looked back he saw Ann walking toward the door that led out to the waiting room.

"Mrs. Lewis," he called out in her direction.

Ann turned, her big purse swinging by its strap. "Thank you for your time, Doctor," she said down the hallway, and then she walked on through the door.

Heyworth started after her, but he stopped after a few steps and watched Ann's shadow pass behind the opaque pane over the reception-ist's desk. When the outer door to his waiting room shut, he turned to Constance. "Do you know anything about this Lewis case?"

"All I know is what's on the forms she filled out when she came in the office."

Heyworth moved back toward his office.

"Her husband is Dr. Shannon's patient, you know," Constance said after him.

"Yes. I saw that," Heyworth replied. "See if you can turn up the medical file on her husband. And be discreet about it."

*   *   *

Ann bumped into a cleaning cart when she came around the corner by the nurses' station. She pushed it away, and when it banged against the wall, two dustpans fell onto the floor. She picked them up and put them back on the cart. If she couldn't get help for her husband, she could at least take care of this little mess.

Jack rolled over when she walked into his room. His pale face was creased on one side from the pillow's seam.

"I just woke up so don't ask me how I'm doing because I don't know yet," he said as she passed to the window.

"I know you just woke up. I can see that. Did Dr. Shannon come by here while I was gone?"

"That's another question you keep asking me."

"Well, did he?"

Jack clutched the rail on the bed's far side and grunted with an effort that propped him only a few inches higher. "No, but I wish he would. I want him to tell me how I'm doing."

Ann looked out at the hospital's opposite wing. The sunlight was sharp against the red brick. She was having a hard time finding words to reassure Jack.

"You said you'd be back soon," he said. "You were gone almost two hours. I thought you'd left me."

"I needed some fresh air." Ann thought this didn't make much sense because it was sweltering outside. "And I got something to eat in the cafeteria, too," she lied.

She saw the potted fern on the window ledge beside her. "This must've been delivered while I was out." She removed the small envelope attached to a frond and read from the note inside, speaking loudly in Jack's direction. 'Get well soon,' it says. 'Love, Mary Lynn.'

Jack took the card and held it with his arm extended so he could read the writing without his bifocals. "I haven't talked to Mary Lynn in six months. We were so close when we were kids. I don't know how things could've changed so much. I wish we were closer now—did I ever tell you that?"

"Several times. You sound like an old man reminiscing."

"I *am* an old man reminiscing." He dropped his arm, and the card fell from his hand and fluttered to the floor, back under the bed. Ann bent down but couldn't reach it. She staggered back when she stood up, reaching for the recliner, and plopped into the chair's mass.

"You okay?" Jack asked.

Her hands were tight on the armrests, her elbows locked stiff. "I'll get Mary Lynn's note later. Don't worry about it right now."

Jack pulled his sheet up over his shoulders, while Ann tilted back in the recliner and shut her eyes. Twenty minutes later, they were both awakened by a gentle rap on the door. A blue-shirted attendant put a food tray on the bedside table. Ann went to Jack's bed when the attendant left and diced the meatloaf into cubes.

"I'll say it again," Jack said, "you don't have to mother me by shoveling food into my mouth."

"And I'll say it again—I like feeding you."

"Well, dadgumit, I'm telling you that I don't like to be fed."

Ann dropped the fork onto the ribbing of the plastic tray. Her hands were on her wide hips. "I'll leave you here all by yourself if you want me to. I certainly don't like sleeping on that cot over there."

"I didn't mean it that way, hon. Sit back down here by me."

"I'm doing more for you around here than just feeding you." She picked up a cube of meatloaf with her fingers and tasted it. "My gosh, they sure put a lot of salt on this. You've got a heart condition, for Pete's sake."

"The meatloaf tastes pretty good to me. You know how I like salt."

"You've got to stop that. You've got to get some better health habits."

She fed him several more bites, and then Jack suddenly stopped chewing and blinked hard several times as his face tightened.

"Your jaw hurts, doesn't it?" she said.

"The pain comes and goes. Mostly it goes."

"Now, how can pain go more than it comes? Explain that to me, Jack."

He began chewing again, gingerly.

"You can't explain that," she said. "You can't explain it at all. Nobody can."

Jack finished eating and rolled over to go to sleep. When Ann finally heard him snoring, she slipped out of the room.

At a pay phone downstairs off the lobby, she called their insurance company. The number was in an area code she didn't recognize and the line rang a half-dozen times until she heard a man's voice. After being passed off three times, Ann spoke to a woman in charge of customer relations.

She asked if Jack could transfer to another hospital under the terms of their insurance agreement. "We want you to be a happy customer," the woman told her politely. When Ann pressed, she was given an answer that amounted to "yes" her husband could transfer, but unfortunately no other local hospital in their network was authorized to treat his condition. She then asked if there was another cardiologist her husband could see in their network, and she was given a quicker answer that amounted to "maybe" and was told to please call another number.

She hung up and went down the hallway to the cafeteria. The odor there was a stale mix of cooked vegetables and meats. Nothing in nature smelled quite like this, and after a half-dozen trips to the cafeteria, Ann felt as if her blouse reeked of it. She moved through the checkout line and sat in a corner, gazing out onto a back street of the medical complex clogged with bulldozers, heavy trucks, and construction cranes. She nibbled on her macaroni and cheese, but had little appetite.

After putting her tray on the food belt near the cafeteria's exit, she walked down another hallway towards the chapel. This corridor was wood-paneled and lined with oil paintings of doctors who had made Mercy Hospital an esteemed institution. Their names were etched at the bottom of the heavy gold frames: Dr. Edward Fleming, 1970–1996, Dr. Thomas Huster, 1950–1964, Dr. Howard Best, 1933–1958, Dr. Ken Reilly, 1936–1950, and on and on.

Ann thought these doctors seemed arrogant. Their heads were held at an angle that implied whatever they touched came out right. The gold picture-frames made her think of how much money doctors made.

At the chapel, there was a prayer box just inside the door. The black panels high in the stained-glass windows spelled out "Ascension of Christ," "Justice," and "Beloved Physician." She went halfway down the aisle and sat in the middle of a row. The altar was ecumenical, the wooden pews squat and square like stone blocks. "Oh, for a Thousand Tongues" droned over the speakers. She knelt on the padded knee rest and asked God for guidance and to be healed of the resentment and disgust she felt toward doctors.

*   *   *

Not long after Ann left his office, Heyworth phoned Marge at the theater.

"How are you?" he asked, trying to sound playful after the heaviness of last night's counseling session and the time he'd spent walking around alone afterward.

"I called earlier."

"I'm just wondering how you're doing. That's why I'm calling."

Marge didn't respond immediately. He heard muffled voices as she spoke to someone else with her hand over the receiver. "I'm fine," she finally said. "Just got back from lunch."

He heard her talking to someone again and the angst he'd felt the previous evening rose up in him. "You didn't go out with that friend of yours today, did you?"

"I did," she said. "But it was with a larger group of about a dozen of us. Today's Colette's birthday, and we all went out for some pretty awful Mexican food."

Heyworth felt his insides churn.

"What?" she said, sensing from his pause that he was bothered. "I told you last night that it was over between me and Sid. Not that there ever was much to be over. I told you the truth about all that. You know that, don't you?"

"Yes." If he continued interrogating Marge she'd close up on him, he realized. "I shouldn't have brought it up. Forget it."

His pager went off. He'd worn one every day for the last twenty-four years, and it never failed to intrude. He looked anxiously at the dial.

"Listen, I'm not sure I can get home early tonight. It's looking like it's going to be around nine o'clock. Maybe we can talk then?"

"Okay," Marge said, her voice tight. "See you then."

CHAPTER 4

Later that same day, Drew Shannon was in his office with Fred Mullenax of AllMed Insurance. Mullenax had been a primary-care physician for two decades before joining AllMed Insurance. His company's patients made up over thirty percent of Mercy Hospital's business; indeed, with Shannon's help, he had worked hard to make this so.

Mullenax, whose wrinkled, coal-colored eyes burned with intensity, raised an issue they'd been discussing for months. "I've talked to several staffers the past few days. It doesn't seem you're getting full cooperation on the changes."

"I've pushed the staff here." Shannon's face was drawn, the circles dark under his eyes. The past months, he'd tightened cost controls and worked on the hospital's department heads to change their habits and philosophies. "Fred, I've done things I never thought I could do."

Mullenax wore a worried frown.

"There's more to be done, I know," Shannon went on. "Yet morale is not good right now, and we had a little shock when your company cut reimbursement rates for some of our doctors."

"We want our business to stay here," Mullenax said.

"I know those cuts had to be made," Shannon added. "They're just going to take a while to digest."

"Ours has been a good alliance for the most part."

"It has," Shannon said, nodding. "I'll revisit the department heads. Let's see if that'll help."

Shannon's intercom came on. His wife Amanda asked him to come see her at her office over in administration. He looked at Mullenax, not wanting to drop the discussion without giving him more assurances. "It's being managed, Fred. Things are changing here, and when we look at the bigger picture, we can see progress. Let's give it time. "

Mullenax stood and Shannon rose with him. But before they reached the door, Probert came in.

He smoothed his black mustache and silvery hair that fell over his ears, looking at Shannon to make sure it was okay to speak frankly with Mullenax there. Probert and the hospital's financial officer, a man named Ty, had a long-running power struggle that required occasional refereeing from Shannon since there was no acting CEO at the hospital.

"Ty came to my office again this morning," he said. "He wants to be involved in every detail on the software installation. That way, his department gets everything first. He even suggested that I report to him."

Annoyed, Shannon took off his glasses and wiped them on his smock. "I'll talk to Ty about it before the executive committee meeting this afternoon."

Shannon moved on toward the administrative wing with Probert and Mullenax walking abreast of him.

"We'll talk later today," Mullenax said to Shannon. "I'll either come by or call."

When Mullenax was gone, Shannon looked at Probert. "We've got to get our new information system up. It's vital."

"I hated to bother you with this," Probert said. "I know you've got a lot going on."

"It's okay. I'll see what I can do to help you with Ty."

"By the way," Probert said, just before he turned off, "This woman came to my office. She said you're treating her husband. She wanted somebody to look into his case."

"Yes," Shannon said. "I have a good idea who that was."

"Older lady. I think she came into my office by mistake."

"I'm addressing her concerns."

"I'm just passing it on," Probert said defensively as he turned in a different direction.

"Thank you."

It was only a short distance over to the administrative wing. Shannon spent his days shuffling between his office where he ran his medical practice and his other office over in administration. This arrangement helped him compartmentalize his duties, and it was also good for appearances since hospital staffers saw him dealing with patients on a daily basis.

Up the hallway, he was joined by a nurse named Ruth whose curly auburn hair spiked out from her cap. She and Shannon had worked together for many years, and he valued her candor and used her as a sounding board.

Ruth matched his strides, and right before she stopped off at a patient's room, she told him, "I just got back from my first vacation in six months. I didn't realize how much I hated this place until I got away for a week." Hearing her say this, Shannon wondered if he'd made a mistake taking the job as medical director. He'd gone into medicine to treat the sick and do good, not to fret over implementing computer systems, or negotiate with HMOs, or try to force people to change. As he walked on, he told himself to stop thinking that way. He'd worked hard to get his joint degree in medicine and business. He was an ace problem solver and he was doing a good job representing other doctors' interests to the HMOs. He liked administration. Despite the strains and long hours, his work was paying off.

He arrived at his wife's office, an interior cubicle lit only by two bronze lamps. Amanda Shannon was head of Ethics and Compliance, a hospital department Drew Shannon had had a hand in creating and staffing.

She was talking on the phone, twisting her silk scarf in her long, slender fingers. Her mouth had a sour look as if something she heard on the line troubled her.

Drew and Amanda Shannon had worked together since she was hired in Utilization Review four years ago. Drew had done much soulsearching when their romance began, torn by his feelings for Amanda and his sense of obligation to his wife of twenty years and their three teenage sons. He finally divorced and then married Amanda before taking a sabbatical two years ago just after he got his business degree.

"I've been talking to a contact at the investment bank," Amanda said when she hung up. "It sounds like the merger talks are moving again."

Drew looked down at her cluttered desk. For months, there had been rumors about the fate of Mercy. He'd quit worrying about the uncertainty of an ownership change at the hospital, about how it would affect the initiatives he had under way. Any merger or sale was for the board of directors to sort through.

"What else are you working on?" he asked.

"Just paperwork," she said, thumbing through a pile. "I don't know how a merger will affect us. We've had an unusual situation here, working together and all. I don't want to lose that."

"We're not going to lose anything."

She held up the front page of that day's newspaper and pointed to the right-hand column. "Did you see this? It's another reason I called you over here."

He took the newspaper. He and Amanda had been following the story of an aggressive federal prosecutor in a neighboring state who'd indicted several hospital administrators and doctors for cozy relationships with HMOs and patient groups, going so far as to probe into perks they'd received, like bonus payments and fishing trips. The article traced the recent progress of the investigation.

"Have you heard anything lately from the FBI?" she asked as he read the story.

"You'll be the first to know if I do. Believe me."

A year earlier, the special-agent-in-charge of the FBI's Madsen bureau, a man named Tom Schiller, had called the hospital's CEO, Dan Houseman, to apprise him of an investigation into health-care fraud. The probe was a joint effort by the state Medicaid fraud units, the American Medical Association, the Inspector General from the Office of Health and Human Services, the state police and various task forces.

Later, Houseman called Agent Schiller back, though at the time no one at the hospital knew about this, or about the names Houseman gave Schiller, several doctors whom he suspected deserved a closer look: Dr. Harrelson, whom AllMed Insurance had already suggested the hospital run off, and several doctors with contracts at outside labs they co-owned. Houseman also mentioned Dr. David Heyworth, who he was having a hard time dealing with as the hospital changed many of its policies to adapt to the managed care.

After Houseman had resigned the winter before, he told Shannon about his contact with the FBI, figuring that as medical director he needed to know. Shannon realized it was dangerous for the hospital to have contact with the FBI, but he didn't show his concern in front of Houseman, nor any disappointment when he heard Heyworth's name, or any of the other names Houseman told him he'd mentioned to the FBI.

Shannon took off his wire-rimmed glasses as he looked up from the newspaper. Amanda nodded as if she knew his thoughts.

Shannon was worried about his vulnerability to an aggressive prosecutor because of his strong ties to AllMed Insurance. When he'd gotten a call months earlier from one of Schiller's deputies, he spoke about the hospital's new measures to heighten internal scrutiny of health-care fraud: Centralization of doctors' billing to better monitor any patterns of abuse, and the newly formed office of Ethics and Compliance to help self-police Mercy's doctors. And to show his cooperation with the crackdown on fraud and also to deflect the FBI's attention to others,

Shannon later copied some files. Among them was the past billing records of Dr. Heyworth.

Shannon stood over Amanda and tried to file it all away into a corner of his mind. "I have paperwork to do myself and then several meetings. I'll see you at home tonight." He turned back from the doorway. "Oh, I forgot to tell you. Heyworth talked to me yesterday about a Quality Assurance citation he got. He thought it was unwarranted."

"He thinks any controls on him are unwarranted."

"Check into it," Shannon said. "It did sound frivolous."

"You mean you didn't defend it?"

"Of course, I did."

"You'd better. I heard he was in an argument up here in administration earlier in the day. He really showed his rear-end. I'm not sure what that was all about."

"Well, I need to respond to him on that citation he got," Shannon said. "Let's give him something on a small matter like this. Later, when the stakes are higher, we can take away something."

Amanda brushed back her blond bangs. "I'll think about it," she said and then she picked up on a topic they'd discussed many times. "But the way that man practices medicine is too risky for the hospital and potentially way too costly, given where we're headed. He pushes too far out on the edge."

"Like I said," Shannon replied. "On his citation, let's give him a small concession. We both know bigger changes are coming."

*   *   *

Later that day, after Heyworth entered his post-op report on Mrs. Rosenbaum's bypass surgery, he thumbed through his mail. A stack of typed correspondence awaited his approval and signature, some of the twenty-five letters he sent out each week to patients and doctors.

When he picked up a CT scan, he brushed the windowsill with it and knocked off his chrome-framed copy of the Hippocratic Oath. As he gathered it off the floor, his eye caught his name in calligraphy across the top. He read the first line of the text, then the second line, down to the phrase he'd always thought to be the oath's essence. *I will prescribe regimen for the good of my patients according to my ability and my judgment and never do harm to anyone.*

He replaced the chrome frame and then examined the CT scan. On the plastic sheet were computerized images of his next patient—a thirty-year-old named Randy Markle who wasn't breathing properly because the aneurysm of his aorta was so large it pressed against his lungs.

There was a shadow in Heyworth's doorway. It was Dr. Sam Tolson, a general surgeon who officed on the same floor. To the extent that he could, Heyworth had mentored Tolson, who was in the early years of his practice. The two men shared a frustration with what was happening in medicine.

"Got a minute?" Tolson asked. The way his smock hung below his knees gave him an unfortunate resemblance to a butcher.

"Not really." Heyworth put down the scan. "But for you, I'll make time."

"I'm in a bind," Tolson said as he stepped inside the office. "I just got a letter from Medicare claiming my practice patterns and billings exceed the peer norm. Any advice?"

"Start a business on the Internet. The government hasn't established peer norms and practice standards for that industry yet."

Tolson ran his fingers through his heavy, dark beard as if something had taken root underneath it. He didn't appreciate the irony of Heyworth's remark, even though the two men had marveled on occasion at the fortunes being made by young entrepreneurs in high-tech fields, and expressed a longing for such freedom and latitude.

"Everything was going along fine," Tolson said, his mouth barely visible under his thick beard. "Or at least I assumed so. Then I get a letter that calls into question billings I turned in two, three, even four years ago."

As Tolson rubbed his eyes with his stubby fingers, Heyworth remembered his own recent tangle with a peer-review group that monitored

Medicare statistics: He'd been served last November with a letter questioning his treatment of two patients who'd died. He'd satisfied the group's inquiries with an exhaustive report noting that the patients' veins were in bad shape by the time each one got through the other specialists. Heyworth had been cleared in the peer review. But now he wondered if the trouble Dr. Tolson was encountering was a sign that such troubles with the Medicare authorities were becoming routine.

"It probably takes the bureaucracy a long time to do a review on the claims," Heyworth said, trying to console him. "And then they have to compare the state and national numbers on code usage. That's probably why they're focusing on such old cases."

Tolson looked up, his eyes bloodshot. "It's frustrating because I've really focused on doing my Medicare billings properly. I even sent my clerk to one of those coding seminars put on by the medical association."

Heyworth reached behind him for a copy of a medical magazine from the bookshelf. "That ad is in here somewhere." He found the page he was looking for. "'Conquering Coding—Strategies for Clean Claims and Full Reimbursement,' " he said, his voice sing-song, making the words sound ridiculous. "'Complete explanation of new billing policies, tested guidance to boost your bottom line, clever strategies to lighten your work load'…And here's my favorite line. 'Surgical balancing act: bill the best codes while avoiding fraud.'"

Tolson peered through his bushy eyebrows. "You wouldn't think this was amusing if it was happening to you."

"I'm not amused at all. Not a damn bit." Heyworth pealed through the magazine's pages, flicking his wrist. "Just look at this. Here's an ad for a publication that claims it's devoted to getting your fair share of Medicare reimbursement dollars. Whatever that means."

"You should talk," Tolson said. "Most of your patients are on Medicare."

"I know. I spend too much energy worrying over reimbursements and regulations."

"Constance knows a lot about this sort of stuff. Maybe she can help me. I wanted to clear it with you first."

"She deserves a Purple Heart for her battles with the bureaucracy," Heyworth said and then he turned to the grainy picture of his father on his desk.

The photograph had been taken twelve years earlier when several hundred people gathered at a baseball field in San Belladro, a town three hundred miles west of Madsen, to honor his father upon his retirement as a general practitioner. The old man stood underneath a banner that read "Doc Heyworth Day."

"My father said it would come to this for doctors," Heyworth said. "He had posters in his waiting room back in the nineteen-sixties that opposed Medicare. He would go on and on at the dinner table about how it would slowly strangle medicine. His ranting about stuff like that drove my mother nuts, which I suppose is the same thing I've done to my wife, now that I think about it. It's odd how we can become our parents."

"I just don't know what I'm going to do about getting all these records together," Tolson said. "It'll take forever, and I'm not really sure what they're after."

"Well, I'm sorry you're in a spot," Heyworth said as his phone rang. "But the bureaucrats are the judge and the jury when it comes to medical records. I'll ask Constance to call your office manager about it."

Tolson waved with a beaten-down farewell as Heyworth picked up the line.

The nurse, calling from down in Heyworth's operating room, told him it was taking longer to prep Mr. Markle for surgery than expected. Heyworth hung up and reached for the CT scans of the patient's chest, but before he could review them again, Constance came in and plopped a notebook in front of him: The pages were neatly bound, fresh off a computer. "Fred Mullenax from AllMed Insurance just dropped this off. I told him you were busy. He said he'd be back in a few minutes."

"Not now," Heyworth said.

"It's the second time he's come by this week. I've put him off more times this summer than I've put off my mother-in-law's visit." Constance talked on as Heyworth studied the CT scans. "She wants to come down here in the summer's heat for some reason. She never invites us up to Maine. I think she worries her house isn't big enough or nice enough, but the cool air there would be really good for my son's asthma."

"I have a friend with a house in Maine. Bar Harbor. How far is she—?"

"Oh, I couldn't do that, Doctor. I wouldn't want to impose. That's nice of you, though."

Heyworth told Constance about Dr. Tolson's request and she agreed to help. Then he realized he could use the extra time the delay prepping Mr. Markle gave him.

After he told her to go get Mullenax, Heyworth scanned the notebook's pages. Every patient, doctor, test, and surgery covered by the insurance company was represented by a data point, a graph, a chart of some sort. Six heart surgeons, including him, were vying for AllMed Insurance's business in the Madsen area, and from a cursory look at the data, Heyworth confirmed what he'd expected: his treatment patterns meant he wasn't likely to keep the business.

There was an insistent knock on the door, and Fred Mullenax came in, his dark eyes gleaming on his time-worn face. While still seated, Heyworth reached over his desk to shake Mullenax's hand, but the doctor's grip missed slightly and the two men disengaged awkwardly.

"You've seen our report," Mullenax said.

"Skimmed it just now." Heyworth lifted the CT scan to the light and rotated the dark plastic sheet to see the images of Mr. Markle's chest better. He looked through one eye and then the other as if winking.

"I wanted to stop by to see you, Doctor." Mullenax was also looking in the direction Heyworth gazed. "Your utilization numbers are a bit better over the past quarter."

"If so, it was unintentional."

"Well, I wouldn't be doing my job for AllMed if I didn't come by and discuss them."

Mullenax was still standing, and Heyworth motioned for him to sit. The chair's armrests cramped Mullenax and he rocked side to side, straightening his suit coat.

"Now, about my numbers," Heyworth said. "There's a time lag in your data. I'm not doing anything differently with my patients. You probably won't like my stats in the next report."

"That's not necessarily true."

Heyworth wanted to shift the conversation away from his performance to what Mullenax's insurance company was doing. He had an instinct for changing the terms of discussion, for penetrating to the core of things. "I read in the hospital newsletter here that your company now covers almost thirty percent of the patients here. The new managed care contract's all on a capitated rate, isn't it?"

Mullenax nodded.

"I'm against paying a flat fee per patient no matter what treatment they might need," Heyworth said. "It turns the incentives in hospitals against patients. Imagine a grocery store that charges a flat fee for each customer. How many people would wind up getting noodles and how many would get steak?"

"A hospital isn't a grocery store, Doctor."

"These types of arrangements stand human nature on its head. They give doctors an incentive to provide less treatment than the patient requires. No other profession has incentives like these. It doesn't make sense."

"The business community likes these capitated plans. It holds down their costs."

"Well, screw the business community! It's still a stupid practice."

Mullenax glanced away, then back. "I didn't come here to be confrontational, Dr. Heyworth. You should think of our insurance company as your consultant and partner. We're putting together a board of surgeons to review our protocols and procedures. We could use more input from doctors like you."

Heyworth stared at Mullenax, at the pink flesh spilling over his stiff shirt collar. If he accepted the invitation, he'd be able to convey his ideas about the practice of medicine to the insurance company. But this wasn't likely to change anything, and besides, his participation could compromise his principles or his care. "I just gave you my input," he said.

"This isn't just another committee," Mullenax added. "This oversight board determines our policies, and you'll work with some quality people. It'll help you keep your ear to the ground as things evolve in health care."

"My ear's to the ground already."

"Knock, knock," Constance said as she barged in. She had a thick file in her hand. "I'm sorry to interrupt, gentlemen. But there's a call on line one. It's a doctor down in Argentina."

Heyworth took the file on the Argentine patient from her and then looked at Mullenax. "This is private," he said.

Constance escorted Mullenax out and closed the door.

The Argentine doctor had a thick Spanish accent. Heyworth examined the file and told him his patient needed a heart aneurysm removed. After more discussion Heyworth agreed to treat the patient, who would fly to Madsen in six days. He laid out his payment terms for foreign patients: half the bill paid up front. The doctor agreed, and Heyworth put the line on hold and scribbled a note for Constance.

Heyworth opened his door, and as Mullenax came back in, he discreetly slipped the message to Constance. It read, "Line 1 needs wiring instructions."

"You miss practicing medicine?" he asked Mullenax as the two men sat down.

"Wouldn't go back for anything." Mullenax smiled thinly, exposing his tiny, perfect teeth. "You're not interested in a job like this, are you? Who knows? Maybe someday?"

"Never. But I am astonished at how many doctors these days say they are interested in an administrative job. It seems fewer and fewer people want to treat patients, in part because of the hassles created by people like you."

Constance came back in, short of breath. "I'm so sorry, gentlemen," she said, handing Heyworth another file. "It's another overseas call. This one's from France but she speaks better English than the last doctor."

"I know," Mullenax said grumpily to Heyworth as Constance led him out. "You need your privacy."

This call was about complications with a French patient. Heyworth went over the case with the head doctor and then gave her detailed instructions. The instant he hung up the phone, Constance opened his door.

"Mullenax is gone," she announced.

"Good."

"I gave him a cup of coffee and tried to keep him near the kitchen, but he wandered around the office. He asked how many staffers we had now. Who did what, exactly." She looked away as Heyworth's wary mood registered on her. "Of course he asked about your foreign patients."

"What about them?"

"What percentage of your business comes from overseas. What rates you charge them. Any problems you have with them. I guess the phone calls stirred his interest."

Heyworth had built his base of foreign patients by publishing articles and speaking at conferences overseas. He was among the best in the world at treating thoracic aortic aneurysms. While most doctors were growing increasingly dependent on local patients controlled by HMOs and Medicare, Heyworth's foreign patients provided him an additional revenue stream. They were one of his last sources of autonomy as a doctor.

Heyworth came around his desk, headed to surgery. "He's probably interested in my foreign patients because they give him an idea of the costs I might run up on patients controlled by his insurance company."

"Well, I told him that if he wanted more information he'd have to talk to you."

"Oh," he said with a disgusted wave. "He can find out virtually anything about my practice anyway if he wants to know. I just wish he'd be up front about it."

*　　*　　*

Early that evening, Heyworth was back at his desk, remembering the warm smile on the elder Mr. Markle's face after the four-hour operation on his son. ("Hit a home run," Heyworth had told him. "Now all we have to do is get your son around the bases.") He stared out at the masts of the distant skyscrapers and thought of Marge and then tried to focus on his work.

A crumpled white tissue that Ann Lewis had left during her visit was still on his desk. The sight of it made him wonder what was happening to her and to her sick husband.

In his line of vision there was a silver canister with the angiogram of a patient named Bess Koshmarian inside it. Even though Constance had moved the woman's surgery to tomorrow morning, he needed to review her tape. He tried to pry open the canister, but the lid was stuck. His knuckles whitened as he tried again. He clenched his front teeth, and in a burst he swiveled and hurled the canister against the wall.

Constance came in, alarmed by the exploding sound. A roll of film lay in a twisted clump beside the severed halves of the canister.

"I couldn't get the damn thing open," he said, looking at the floor.

Constance bent to pick up the debris, but Heyworth held his hand up, signaling her to stop. He reloaded the film in the canister and sat down, rubbing his temples with his fingertips.

Constance took the canister off his desk and tightened the lid. "I'd say poor Mrs. Koshmarian's angiogram here got bounced around pretty good."

"I need to go see her. She's in surgery first thing tomorrow."

"I hate to even bring this up now," Constance said, wincing. But she'd learned to dump bad news on him all at once because he didn't get much more upset over three or four things gone wrong than he did over one. "We've got a small problem with Mr. Reedy's case. I need you to talk to the insurance company first thing tomorrow. We can't seem to get them to agree that he needs treatment, and you have a way of persuading them."

"Don't put me on the line with another hourly-wage employee at the insurance company. If I have to cajole somebody else who doesn't know much about medicine, it had better at least be somebody who can make a decision."

"Yes, sir," she said, backing to the door. "I'm going home in about ten minutes. You staying late?"

He stared blankly at his desk, and then, as if he'd been far away, he said in an overloud tone, "Do you have anything else for me?"

"Mrs. Pickell told Laney she's worried she's being sent home too soon. She says she hears stories."

"Unbelievable," he replied, rising. "We spent five hours operating on Mrs. Pickell. She arrested while she was on the operating table. I've never been so exhausted as I was after that surgery, and now she's having to worry about *that*."

He followed Constance out and waited in the hall as she gathered her purse and briefcase in her office. They took the elevator down, and Heyworth walked her to the parking deck. It was unusual for him to see Constance off like this, but he sometimes worried, particularly when he felt overwhelmed, about losing her. He knew he'd driven off his previous office manager with his demands.

"I really appreciate you," he said, patting her back.

"Why, thanks, Doctor," she said, looking sheepish.

"Are things okay with you? I mean at home and all—with your son and his new school."

"I'm managing. But thanks for asking. Are things okay with you?"

"They're so-so," he said. "Aline is going off to college."

"Yeah. You having a hard time with it?"

"I'm having family problems in general." He knew Constance, with her intuitions, had a good idea exactly what he was referring to.

"I'm sorry. I hope it all works out for you, Doctor."

Heyworth said good night. Then he turned and headed back across the walkway.

It was almost seven o'clock. Hospitals, like police stations and public plazas, never close down, they just grow still for a time. Except for the late-shift nurses and white-shirted moppers, the halls of Mercy, with their bright lights and faint smell of disinfectant, were empty.

At the nurses' station, Heyworth was joined by Laney. Her long chestnut hair, typically tucked under her cap when she assisted him in surgery, hung down her back. Further down the hall, they stopped outside a patient's room.

"This is Mrs. Koshmarian," Laney said, briefing him. "She's quite nervous about her operation." She handed him a clipboard, and after Heyworth studied the data on the pages, he opened the door.

Bess Koshmarian, a small-boned woman wearing a pink robe, was on the phone. When she saw them she lowered her voice. "I've got to go now," she said, as if the Mafia had arrived. She turned to Heyworth. Her face was pruney from age and overexposure to the sun.

"How you doing, sweetheart?" he said. "Good to see you."

She smiled and said, "Hi, Doctor," and pointed at the table behind him. "I was doing better until I read that thing over there."

Heyworth recognized the disclosure form—he always had his office print it on bright-pink paper. "Oh, that. Laney brought that by, didn't she?"

"Doctor, the part in the form about the chance of paralysis rattled me, and I'm not easily rattled, I'll tell you that right now."

He laid the sheet flat on the chair's armrest. "This is a serious operation," he said to her. "When I do it, I want us to understand each other. I don't want any surprises and neither do you. This is an extra form I want my patients to read and sign, that's all."

Mrs. Koshmarian took the pen Laney handed her. "There," she said as she scribbled her name. "I'm all yours. Signed and sealed."

Heyworth put the form in his top pocket, and when he lowered his hand, she clutched it and weaved her thin fingers between his. He felt her palm tremble slightly.

"I pray that God will guide your hand, Doctor," she said, looking up.

"Me too." Unless pressed, he didn't tell his patients he wasn't religious.

"I was talking to my daughter when you came in. She wants a guarantee."

"Guarantee? There are no guarantees on this surgery. You're really going to have to fight after this procedure. Can you do that for me?"

Mrs. Koshmarian bent over and touched her palms to the floor and counted aloud to five. Wisps of gray hair flew out from her bird-like head when she straightened up. "How many of your patients can do that? I was a dancer, and I'm a battler, too. I guarantee that."

"Good." He grinned and hugged her, resting his chin on the crest of her head. "And I guarantee I'll do my best in the operating room."

After he and Laney left the room, a plump dark-haired nurse ran up to them. "Mrs. Koshmarian's pulse rate spiked up to 140," the nurse said, almost breathless. "I just noticed it on the heart monitor down the hall. Is she okay?"

"She's fine. Just calm down," Laney told the nurse. "Mrs. Koshmarian was just reading the release form for the operation. It's a common reaction. It happens fairly often. You can go back to your station. It's okay."

Heyworth and Laney went on up the hallway to see more patients of his. Near the nurses' station, an elderly man shuffled toward them, pushing his IV pole on rollers. As Heyworth watched the man pass by, he caught Laney's eye.

"Be especially gentle with Mrs. Koshmarian when you open her up tomorrow morning," he said. "She's been through a lot, and she's more frail than most, no matter what she thinks." Then he realized Laney might take his comment the wrong way. "Not that you aren't gentle with every patient in the operating room."

Laney smiled. "A stealth surgery, that's what you're talking about, isn't it, Doctor? We'll just slip in there undetected, fix her little ole aorta, and then slip right out as if nothing at all happened."

Heyworth gave a throaty chuckle. "Yes, if you can arrange it, that would be a really nice miracle, wouldn't it?"

*   *   *

Back at his office, Heyworth saw a message from Constance that his father had phoned. He called back, but there was no answer.

Lloyd Heyworth had been lonely since his wife died last summer. Heyworth had invited him to come to Madsen several times the past year, but between the seven-hour drive and his father's dislike of planes there'd been no visit. The last time they'd spoken Lloyd had asked him to come to out to his San Belladro ranch and go with him to the cemetery where Heyworth's mother and other relatives of his were buried.

Heyworth's youth had been dominated by his father. As a boy, he hung around Lloyd's office, became used to patients showing up at their house at odd hours of the day and night, watched his dad deliver babies, once out in a peach orchard. Lloyd Heyworth was particularly skilled at diagnosing illnesses. He had, when necessary, referred his patients to the best doctors at the most prestigious hospitals in the cities. Doctors like his son had become.

Heyworth put away the message slip and gathered his briefcase, his empty Tupperware bowl. He knew his father was proud of him, and if he left medicine earlier than he'd planned, he wanted him to understand. He didn't live for his father's approval, but it was important to him.

He drove his black sedan out onto the freeway, then through the quiet back streets of the Morningside neighborhood, under the canopies of the old oak trees. It was just past eight-thirty, with only a trace of light in the sky.

At his house, Marge was in the kitchen. She wore gray capri pants and a lime-green blouse. Her hair was curled, and she'd placed fresh-cut roses on the kitchen's island like a peace offering.

"Hello," he said as he came to her. "You look great."

"Thanks." She gave him a quick hug.

"How was your day?"

"Okay. Not bad." She went to the refrigerator and pulled out sliced turkey, lettuce, tomatoes.

"Where's Aline?"

"Out with friends," Marge said. "She doesn't have many more nights with them before she goes away."

Heyworth went to the study to check his mail. A few minutes later, Marge carried in an oversized plate loaded with turkey sandwiches, thin wedges of cheese and chutney spread for the gourmet crackers. She put the food on the ottoman and sat on the floor, chewing a morsel of the cheese.

"We had quite a talk last night," she said. "How are you feeling about it?"

"What do you think about things?" He watched her reach for a cherry tomato, but she didn't reply. He answered himself. "I believe we can reconnect rather quickly if we try."

"You think so?" she said. She pushed back a lock of hair. "We didn't talk about our sex life last night. It's been bothering me. Vanessa thinks we should discuss it."

He picked up his sandwich, thinking of last night, of how she'd mentioned her interest in other men. "To tell you the truth, I don't have any energy left for sex these days."

"You never told me that."

"I know. It just seems like I've lost interest."

"Maybe you've just lost interest in me."

"It's not you, hon," he said. "I feel sapped by the struggles of my work. It's been getting worse the last few years."

"We don't have sex much, unless I initiate it, and I don't do that very often, I admit. And when we do have sex it seems like we're not all there, not totally in the moment. You're sure there's been no one else for you?"

"How could you think that? I feel guilty enough about neglecting you for my work. An affair would only make me feel worse."

Marge looked away, then back at him with hurt in her eyes. "I don't want to burden you with guilt, David, but do you realize you didn't say you wouldn't have an affair because you loved me?"

"You know that's what I meant," he said remorsefully.

"No. I don't know that, really."

They each looked at the floor. Marge had her arms tight around her folded legs and Heyworth had put down his sandwich.

"I'm trying to tell you how I feel about sex," he finally said. "I know I haven't been very attentive. I love you, Marge."

"Sex is part of the problem. But it's more than that. I feel trapped here. We built this life together, yet somewhere along the way I feel as if I've gotten lost."

Heyworth leaned over his plate. "What can we do to change that?"

"Talking like this helps. But there's more," she said. "Last night, I mentioned going on an adventure. I need to be rattled loose or something." Her lips were pinched tight. "And I've thought of quitting my fund-raising work at the theater and getting back into drawing and painting. I need to find new ways to express myself."

Heyworth nodded. He'd seen new charcoal pencils on the shelves of the study and her old easels rearranged in the hall closet. "Maybe you can turn the bedroom upstairs into a work space. It will be peaceful up there when Aline leaves."

Marge took up a cracker and spread chutney on it. Her eyes were careworn, almost teary, and she seemed withdrawn as if afraid of what else she might say.

Heyworth sensed her frailty and didn't want her to pull back. His reserve dropped away. "You know, I've had thoughts of doing something very different with my life, too," he said.

She put a half-eaten cracker back on the tray and sat upright, crossing her legs under her. "Like what?"

"Like quitting medicine." He leaned his head back against the chair. "Soon," he added.

"How long have you been seriously thinking about this?" she asked, her voice sounding surprised and troubled.

"It's been on my mind for quite a while. I think about it more all the time. It would be better if I could wait a few years, but I'm not sure I can."

"I can't believe we've grown so far apart that you haven't shared this with me."

"The clues have been there. But I guess you haven't noticed them."

Marge moved to the couch, facing him. "I'm not sure how to take this…or what it means for us."

"I hope you'd see such a change positively."

She looked hard at him. Then her eyes softened. "Medicine is your whole life, David. What will you do with yourself?"

"There are other things I can do. I'll find other purposes for my life. I think we have enough money saved to live fairly comfortably. Until I find something else."

He had a self-made man's confidence that he could create himself anew. He'd recently made a list in his diary of their assets: home equity, four-hundred fifty-thousand dollars; several million in investments; a retirement plan and 401(k), plus another million in accounts receivable, less write-offs for uncollectible money from Medicare and charity cases. It was enough capital to let him try something new, if he so chose.

"Listen," he said, touching her hand. "I've been so unhappy the past few years because I feel like my autonomy has been under attack in my work. As you know, it's been hard for me to find much peace, much less to experience anything approaching joy. I'm only now realizing how much it's affected our marriage."

"Don't leave medicine for me, David. I don't want that."

"That's not what I'm saying. When I leave, it'll be for me. On my own terms."

She eased back into the couch. Heyworth tried to read her thoughts in her eyes. "Marge, don't talk about this to anyone," he said, "not even Aline. I want to tell her when I finally decide. Besides, I've got to get my mind around leaving my practice and that could take a while longer."

"Now you sound ambivalent."

"I'm still sorting it out. It's gut-wrenching for me."

Marge looked past him, gazing at the pattern in the carpet. Then she came to his chair and stood over him. "You're not going to sleep in the guest bedroom again tonight, are you?"

"No, I want to sleep with you. But I'm going to stay up a little while. I'm keyed up from work."

She touched him tenderly on his cheek. "Listen for Aline to come in."

After Marge left the room, Heyworth heard Cab whining in the kitchen and let him out the back door. There was the sound of an engine outside, and he saw headlights swing low across the lawn, but the car was just turning around in the driveway. He wished Aline would come home before he went to bed.

In his study, he got out the paper, "Twelve-Year Operative Experience with 307 Thoracic Aortic Aneurysm Surgeries" and worked for a half-hour on it. When he finally undressed and crawled into bed next to Marge, she was asleep. He turned on the tiny light clipped onto his Sherlock Holmes mystery and read a chapter. The pitter-patter of squirrels scampering on the slate roof at the house's far end made him think for a moment that Aline was coming in the back door.

Heyworth went to sleep and dreamed that a cloth sack was held over his face. He awakened sweaty and chilled and snuggled into

Marge's shoulder, but when he nodded back off, he had much the same dream again.

At five-thirty, he was up. The dawn was gray, smothered by clouds. In the kitchen, he read the city newspaper and then yesterday's *Wall Street Journal*.

Marge came in around six o'clock, wrapped in her turquoise kimono. She put a packet of fancy coffee into the coffeemaker.

"You're not going running this morning? That's two days in a row you've missed."

"Not up to it today," he said. "Didn't sleep well."

"Was it our conversation last night?"

"Partly. And partly it's a case at the hospital that's on my mind."

"Of course." Marge rubbed her eyes. "I didn't sleep well either, and now that I'm up, I'm feeling really, really tired. What time did Aline get home?"

"She wasn't in yet when I came to bed."

Heyworth had two cups of coffee while Marge made his tuna salad and packed it up for him. He pulled out of the driveway fifteen minutes earlier than usual. The sun was rising through the haze, and traffic was heavy because there'd been a wreck on Union Street, near the hospital.

At his office, Constance was at the cubicle where the receptionist usually sat, sipping ice water, working her way through a pile of paperwork.

"Morning," Heyworth said when he came in.

"How are you? I took care of the trouble we were having between Mr. Reedy and the insurance company. You know, the approval we needed at the insurance company. We discussed it last night."

"Yes," he said, remembering. He walked slowly past the front desk, twisting his head in circles, working out a crimp in his neck.

"You all right this morning?" Constance called out as he went down the hallway. "I can get you some coffee."

"That's okay," he replied. "Had plenty."

"You need to head down to the O.R. in an hour," she shouted just before he stepped into his office. "Mrs. Koshmarian will be waiting. Plus, you have a transplant this afternoon."

Heyworth scanned his e-mail: a reminder from the administration about a peer-review meeting, new guidelines from the FDA on relevant drugs, a note from a colleague in Boston about a scientific paper on coronary bypass. He looked out at the horizon, now sharp blue with the haze burned off.

Constance came in and slid a thick file in front of him. She crossed her arms high on her chest triumphantly. Heyworth saw that the folder was Jack Lewis's patient file.

"I came in early to finish this up," she said. "I figured you probably worried about the case all night."

"It wasn't the only thing on my mind."

He opened the file, looking at Shannon's work-up of the patient, the transcript of the consultation, the report from the cath lab that was the essence of the patient for a heart surgeon. What he saw gave him cause to question Shannon's judgment. He wanted more information about the Lewis case.

"The angiogram isn't in there," Constance said. "I'll go get it in a little while, but I want to be here when the other staffers come in this morning. I need to give them some instructions to start the day."

Heyworth stood. "You go on about your business. I'll be right back."

He crossed over to the hospital, and up on the second floor, he discovered the door to the records room was locked. He was standing there jiggling the knob—he didn't know the security code required to open it—when he sensed someone approaching behind him. It was Ruth, the curly auburn-haired nurse who was a confidante of Drew Shannon's.

"Surprised to see you up here, Doctor," she said.

"I'm doing some of my own legwork this morning." He looked past her at the door. "The lock, it's new, isn't it?"

"Concerns about the confidentiality of patient files. But it's not a new lock. It's been here quite a while." Ruth stepped up and punched in the security code. "Some of you doctors don't know half the stuff that goes on around here. You people get into your own little world and can't, or won't, see out."

Ruth unlocked the door and walked to the far end of the long, narrow room. Heyworth followed her in. Racks of tin canisters were stored in rows like books, holding the cinefilm records of the hospital's patients going back five years. Near the front wall, amidst the films of current patients, Heyworth spotted the silver canister with Jack Lewis's name on it.

"Close the door behind you when you leave," Ruth said.

In the dark, windowless copy room down the hall from his office, Heyworth fished the canister from the pocket of his smock and loaded the cinefilm onto his projector. The murky-white images of Jack Lewis's heart flickered on the screen and the frames showed narrowings on the top left main artery and down the left anterior descending artery. The diagnosis involved judgment, but to Heyworth's eye three-quarters of the diameter of both arteries were blocked.

CHAPTER 5

The morning of the Lewises' third day at the hospital, Jack lay in bed watching TV while Ann read *Sunset* magazine in the recliner. The food tray with the remains of his low-fat, low-sodium breakfast was on the bedside table, and the cot she'd slept on was pushed to the wall.

"I'm bored," Jack said. His coloring was a rosier than normal because mid-morning was his best time. "How much TV can one man watch?"

"What do you expect for entertainment around here? Dancing girls?" Ann shimmied her shoulders. "You want me to do a little number for you?"

"Oh hush," he said. "Why don't you go down to the gift shop and get me a news magazine or a *Popular Mechanics* or a *Golf Digest*. I need something else to read besides one of your magazines about how to make a better fruit salad."

"You're awfully spry this morning. Which magazine do you want?"

"All of them." His eyes followed Ann as she passed by the bed. "You know, you don't have to stay here with me tonight."

"We'll see how the day goes."

He frowned. "It'll do you good to get out of the hospital. You'll be only an hour away, and you can check on Ibi while you're home."

"Ibi's fine at the kennel," Ann said. She didn't like the idea of leaving Jack alone in the hospital overnight. "Besides, it's an hour and fifteen minutes door-to-door. An hour and a half if traffic is bad. And traffic is usually bad."

"It won't kill me to stay here by myself for one night," Jack said.

"I'll think about it. There are hotels nearby. We'll see."

"If you go to a hotel at least you can sleep on a decent bed, instead of that cot."

"I said we'll see, Jack. We'll see means we'll see."

She went down to the lobby and bought magazines and some tooth-paste in the gift shop. On her way back, she stopped at the pay phones and dialed Neal's number. She'd promised to call him. When he answered, it turned out he was on the other line talking to Jack.

"I'll hold until you finish your conversation with him," she said. "And I'll call you back if I get cut off." She watched a hospital attendant mop the tile floor in long, looping swaths. A minute later, Neal clicked onto her line.

"How are you, Mother?"

"Fine. But your father hasn't taken his heart condition very seriously; you know how he can be. His fall on the patio last week seemed to get his attention, finally."

"He sounds like he's in pretty fair spirits, considering. As best as I can tell."

"Well, you can't tell very much from up there in Seattle." She huddled back into the phone booth as the mopper passed behind her. "I'm still having a hard time figuring out how he's really doing. He's a bit more chipper this morning. But this hospital is a strange place, Neal. I tell you I've said a lot of prayers. A lot."

"Mother, have you been outside the hospital at all in the last three days?"

"Your father told you to ask me that."

"No, he didn't. Why are you accusing him like that?"

"Neal, I'm just frustrated—I've been taking it out on him lately, I guess."

"Did you talk to the insurance company?"

"Yeah." She closed her eyes and pressed her forehead against the cold silver plating of the phone's bulkhead. "Neal, don't tell your father what I said about the hospital. In fact, you probably shouldn't talk to him unless I'm there in the room."

"Oh, Mother, really. Come on now."

"I've got to get back up there, Neal. Bye-bye."

*   *   *

While Ann was away, Heyworth came into the room. Jack Lewis looked sideways at him and covered up his bare leg with the sheet.

Jack's broad forehead, deep-set eyes, and thin lips reminded Heyworth of his older brother Jim.

"I've spoken with your wife," the doctor said.

"Okay," Jack said as if he meant, "So?"

Heyworth glanced at the door: He had no face-saving explanation if Drew Shannon walked in, yet he had to examine Jack. With some patients, he relied heavily on the cardiologist's work-up and put less emphasis on an examination, but this case was different.

"I'm a doctor here, Mr. Lewis. Mind if I have a look at you?"

Jack didn't respond right away, as if he hadn't heard Heyworth. "Well, I reckon it won't hurt anything," he finally said as he lowered his hands to his side.

Heyworth turned on the examination light. The bright beam over-head cast Jack's chest a translucent white. Heyworth clutched Jack's ankle to check the pulse and look at the condition of the veins in his legs. He listened through his stethoscope to the throbbing in Jack's carotid arteries to make sure Shannon hadn't missed an obstruction there. He pulled back the sheet and checked the sternum to see if it had been cut before during a heart-bypass operation.

"Are you in pain?" Heyworth asked.

"Some tightness in my chest. Cough that comes and goes. That kind of thing. Better today, but still weak." Jack shifted slowly on the bed. "It seems like my wife is more worried about my troubles than anybody else is around here. I haven't decided if that's good or bad."

Heyworth had seen patients with silent symptoms due to poor circulation—clammy flesh, sallow faces, a flu-like lethargy—who rarely complained about their condition. "What do you think is causing your troubles, Mr. Lewis?"

"My lifestyle, or so my wife says. My past lifestyle, anyway."

"You smoke?"

There were footsteps out in the hall. Heyworth thought another doctor was about to enter. He straightened and stood stiffly as the door opened.

Ann Lewis came in, carrying Jack's magazines. The corners of her mouth turned up in a slight smile of recognition. "Why, Doctor." She came to Jack's bed, blinking her eyes rapidly, adjusting to the bright exam light overhead. "Hello."

"Hi. I won't be much longer."

"Please, take your time."

"You mind shutting the door there?" Heyworth said, looking behind her. He turned back to Jack, who'd raised his knees, making a tent of the white sheet in the middle of the bed. "Do you smoke, Mr. Lewis?"

"I gave up the jewels about six months ago."

"He's talking about those awful Hav-A-Tampa cigars," Ann said. "He had a couple a day."

"Before that I smoked cigarettes for twenty-five years," Jack said. "Started out a pack a week, then a pack a day. I got up to two packs for about a ten-year stretch."

"Don't brag about it," Ann said. "Good grief."

"The doctor asked me." Jack looked at Heyworth. "I smoked Pall Malls. No filters. You could light them from either end. They were little works of art."

Heyworth spoke louder, trying to guide the conversation. "Do you get short of breath, Mr. Lewis?"

"No."

"Are you able to work as much as you were a year ago?"

"I took early retirement about nine months ago. But I admit I can't play golf as much as I could a few months ago."

"Why?"

"Because he gets short of breath," Ann said into the doctor's ear.

Heyworth touched the stitches on Jack's forehead. "What happened here?"

"He fell," Ann said.

"Maybe I need brain surgery to fix it," Jack replied as he stretched his legs out flat.

Ann turned to Heyworth. "He got dizzy last week. Hit his head on the railing around our deck."

"It was darned hot out last week," Jack said.

"It's been hot as Hades all summer," Ann replied. "You've dealt with the heat all your life. Until lately."

Again, there was the sound of footsteps in the hall. The door swung halfway open, and a nurse stood in the entry talking with a colleague. Heyworth put his stethoscope in his lower pocket and stepped away from the bed just before she came in.

"It's time for your medication, Mr. Lewis," the young nurse said. Her name tag read "Nancy," and her head was down over her clipboard. She glanced quickly at Heyworth as if wondering why he was there, and mumbled "hello," as she passed him to get to the bed. "How you doing today, Mr. Lewis?" she added cheerily.

Jack looked at Heyworth, then Ann, then finally the nurse. "I don't really know, to be honest," he replied.

The nurse checked Jack's pulse, temperature and respiration, taking notes.

Heyworth knew little about her loyalties—she was new at the hospital yet very take-charge due to years of experience. Jack's chest was bare, the examination lamp on it like a spotlight. Heyworth had forgotten to turn the light off.

The nurse flicked off the overhead lamp. "Dr. Shannon will be by in a few minutes," she said flatly.

Ann came over to Heyworth and put her arm casually around his waist. "It was so good of you come by and see us," she said. "It's always great to see old friends," she added, moving Heyworth toward the door.

The nurse entered the data on her clipboard onto a computer in a recess just outside the doorway, keeping an eye out for Shannon. Heyworth watched her move up the hallway. Not too far ahead, he picked out the doctor's gaunt visage and gray-blond hair.

"I think I'd better get going," he said to Ann.

He passed quickly by the room Shannon had entered.

*   *   *

When Ann came back to the room, Jack settled onto his side, facing her.

"Would you like some Coke?" she asked.

"I didn't know you had a doctor friend here."

"I ran into him in the hallway. I recognized him from my nurses' training way back when."

Jack yawned deeply, closing his eyes for several seconds. "That was a long time ago. You've got a good memory."

"About some things I do."

"Well, apparently I don't. Or I'm losing my memory, along with my mind. What was that doctor's name? I don't think I asked him, and he never did say."

"Didn't you see his name on his smock?" she said, though she knew the name tag had been obscured by the papers sticking out of Heyworth's top pocket. She rummaged in the tiny closet for a can of Coke she'd stored there the day before.

"Why was that doctor examining me?" Jack asked.

"Because I asked him to," she said, looking back. "As a favor."

"Why?"

"What do you mean, 'Why?' That's what doctors do."

"Well, he came in, and then you came back in, and then the nurse showed up. In all that coming and going, all I got out of him was that he was a friend of yours. Didn't even get his name."

She worried that Jack might repeat Heyworth's name to Shannon when he came to the room. She remembered the name of one of the retired doctors in the oil portraits off the hospital's main lobby. "Fleming," she said. "His name is Dr. Fleming." She shut the closet door. "I thought we had a Coke in here, but we don't. I'll go down to the cafeteria and get us something to drink after Dr. Shannon comes by."

"Just bring me a good ole glass of tap water for now," Jack said. "Then come over here and sit with me and be still for a while."

She handed him the magazines she'd bought for him.

"Just put them down there," he said, his eyelids heavy. "I'll look at them later. I've gotten tired all of a sudden."

*   *   *

Heyworth returned to the tiny room that housed his projector. He wanted to re-check what he'd seen—it was one more way of being thorough. He rewound the tape to the identifier label to make sure the name on it was correct: It was indeed an angiogram of Jack Lewis's heart, taken within the last week.

Heyworth again saw a three-quarters narrowing of the two arteries on the angiogram, and, apparently, he realized, Shannon saw only a narrowing of one-third or so, a condition less critical. Or maybe Shannon wanted to see only an insignificant blockage, Heyworth thought. He didn't relish having to challenge Shannon. But if he didn't do what he thought was right, he'd have to live with the consequences, including perhaps Jack Lewis's premature death.

"Dr. Eddington is here to see you," Constance told him just outside the door to his office.

"Who?"

"Eddington, the young gastrointerologist. You must see him occasionally in the halls. He says he wants to talk about a private matter."

"I don't know Dr. Eddington well enough to discuss anything of a private nature."

"He's insistent that he see you right away. That's all he'll tell me."

"Give me a few minutes."

Heyworth picked up the X-rays of Jack Lewis's chest and held the sheet to the light, checking for enlargement and other abnormalities.

There was a knock on the door and Heyworth saw Dr. Eddington's youthful, flat face and too-wide eyes pop into view.

"Sorry to bother you like this," Eddington said, his voice sincere.

Heyworth put down Jack Lewis's X-rays. "You've strayed a long way to come here. Your office is over in the Terry Building, isn't it?"

"Actually I'm in the Lawrence Building. But my visit here is a bit unusual, I admit."

"What's on your mind?" Heyworth said, trying to hurry the conversation.

Eddington sat down heavily in the chair opposite Heyworth as if he needed support. "I've heard some disturbing talk around the hospital," he said. "There's word of a crackdown. I've heard whispers of something rather serious happening. That's why I've come to see you."

Heyworth shrugged. "There's always been palace intrigue around this place. I've heard some pretty wild rumors over the years. And there are practical jokers, too. I try not to waste energy on that stuff."

"This rumor is different. I hear law enforcement is involved. The FBI, to be specific."

Heyworth rubbed his chin, annoyed by the cat-and-mouse nature of the discussion. "You didn't come all the way over here to tell me about some random rumor, I know that."

"Not exactly, Doctor," Eddington said, his voice getting lower as if he were troubled over what he had to say. "I'm here because I heard your name specifically mentioned in connection with all this."

Heyworth leaned into his desk. "What do you mean, exactly?"

"I hear the entire med center is being investigated for health care fraud. That includes this hospital."

Heyworth had joked to Dr. Tolson that when he read the papers lately he got the sense that the federal government was investigating almost everyone in health care for fraud.

"Some of these violations are pretty technical, I hear," Eddington went on. "The rumor is that the hospital administration may be using this investigation as a pretext to go after certain people."

Heyworth didn't flinch, but his mind raced. His documentation was good, he thought. He worked at it, unlike some doctors who used poor record-keeping to cut corners. But, my God, there were hundreds of Medicare billing codes he was responsible for—the book of regulations was tens of thousands of pages thick—and they were constantly changing.

"I just wanted to give you a heads-up on all this, that's all," Eddington said.

Heyworth stared past him and thought about the hotline number now put on statements to Medicare patients encouraging them to report fraud. He'd made judgments that could be questioned, he realized. He put a tube in a patient and called it a pericardostomy, reimbursable by Medicare for hundreds of dollars. On another sicker patient, he coded the procedure as a pericardial window, reimbursable for thousands of dollars. And his tinkering with defibrillators probably violated Medicare protocol of some sort. He couldn't ask mother-may-I each time he faced a decision, and besides the regulations were too complex and ambiguous. Even the most scrupulous doctor could get nailed for something, especially if somebody had a mind to get him.

"Doctor," Eddington said, speaking louder to get Heyworth's attention. "I don't mean harm by telling you this. I feel like I know you, at least by reputation anyway. Some people around here see you as a role model."

Heyworth was in no frame of mind for small talk or flattery. "I'm sure you mean well," he said. "Now excuse me. Please."

After Eddington left, Constance came in, her eyebrows arched and tense. "Dr. Eddington looked upset. Is there anything I should do to follow up on your conversation with him?"

"No," Heyworth snapped.

She stepped back, stung.

"Wait a minute," he said. "I'm sorry." He circled around her and closed the door. Then he sat on the front of his desk, his eyes level with hers. "Constance, have you heard any rumors around here of a crackdown?"

"It seems the hospital or the insurance companies are always cracking down on someone or something."

"I'm talking about a different type of crackdown. Dr. Eddington claims to know of an FBI investigation going on at the med center. You read in the newspapers about these things at other places."

"You know how the rumors can be at the hospital. But I can poke around to see if there's any new talk."

"No." He looked up at the ceiling, wondering how to proceed. "Do you think Dr. Eddington's trustworthy?"

"I've had lunch a time or two with his office manager. She doesn't particularly like him, but I don't remember why. I could ask—"

"Don't ask anybody anything. Not now." Heyworth went behind his desk and rustled some papers, trying not to seem too rattled. "Let's just leave it alone."

"Okay, Doctor," Constance said with a shrug. Then she moved on to the next item of business. "Laney called. You need to be down in the operating room in an hour for the transplant."

Heyworth noted the time. "What's taking them so long down there?"

"Apparently the heart hasn't arrived yet."

"Keep me informed," he said. "And, Constance, not a word about our conversation to anyone."

∗   ∗   ∗

Forty-five minutes had passed since Heyworth's visit to Jack Lewis's room. Ann paced in and out, scanning the hall in both directions for Shannon. She finally decided he wasn't coming, and told Jack she'd be back soon.

She walked the main corridor. As she ventured deeper into the maze of hallways, gray doors replaced familiar blue ones. She backtracked, then spotted a small palm tree in a sun-drenched window, and recognized this path led over to Heyworth's office building.

She rang the buzzer in his waiting room, but there was no one behind the opaque glass over the counter. Finally, the window slid open. Constance, sitting in momentarily for the receptionist, looked out. Ann told her she needed to see Heyworth, but Constance said he was in surgery. Because it was already late and the heart transplant could take six hours, the best time to see him was tomorrow morning.

Ann retraced her steps to Jack's room. The door was open, and through it she saw Shannon standing beside the bed. The doctor's long fingers probed Jack's chest.

She pulled back, standing outside the doorway, and heard the doctor's voice and then Jack's, more faintly. Had Jack blabbed to Shannon about Heyworth's visit? What *was* he discussing with the doctor? she wondered.

She gathered herself, stepping into the room as if she'd just arrived. Jack was propped up, a look of relief on his face. Shannon smiled when he saw her.

"Mrs. Lewis," he said, touching her elbow. "I just told your husband that I'm releasing him from the hospital tomorrow. He'll continue his medication, of course, but he'll respond just as well at home, and certainly be more comfortable."

Shannon put his stethoscope in his pocket. When Ann looked hard at Jack, the thin smile on his face evaporated.

"What about his chest pains, Dr. Shannon?" she asked. "And he had some jaw pain again yesterday. Did he tell you that?"

Jack cupped his hands around his mouth, making a megaphone. "I had jaw pain yesterday. Everybody hear that?"

"Stop it, Jack," Ann said.

"I finally got some good news. Now you're trying to take it away from me."

Shannon turned away as they argued. He realized Jack's condition could get serious. But he was convinced his diagnosis was technically proper and the risk could be minimized.

"What do you think, Doctor?" Jack asked. "Does my jaw pain change anything?"

Shannon shook his head decisively. "I still think medication is the best way to treat your condition."

"It's her you have to convince," Jack said, pointing to Ann.

Shannon stepped closer to the bed without looking at Ann. "You're going to have a good summer after all, Mr. Lewis."

"You really think so," Jack said.

Shannon nodded.

Behind them, Ann sagged against the recliner. What she was hearing frightened her, but she knew there was little to be gained by confronting Shannon. It would confuse Jack, and any fuss she stirred up would likely complicate matters with Heyworth.

"I might not get by here tomorrow morning before you check out," Shannon said. As medical director, he had a full schedule of administrative appointments.

"It's not necessary, Doctor," Ann said, coming forward. "But we'll have the prescriptions we'll need for his medication, right?"

"One of the nurses will go over them with you. If I don't see you tomorrow, check with my office to schedule a follow-up appointment in a few weeks."

Shannon smiled at Jack, and on his way out, patted Ann's upper arm.

Ann sat in the recliner. When Jack held out his hand, she came to the bed.

"The doctor's very nice," Jack said. "I like him. He's sincere too."

"Don't mistake sincerity for honesty."

Jack's grip on her hand loosened. "What do you mean by that?"

"Nothing. Never mind." She pulled away, but before she sat back down, she turned back to the bed. "You just don't know anything about medicine, Jack. That's all."

"I never said I knew a damned thing about medicine. I've let you be the expert here." He rolled over, his back to her, looking up sideways at the TV. "All I know is that I'm sick of this hospital room, and I want to go home. You can get mad at me for that if you want to."

"I'm not mad, Jack. Hon, I'm sorry. I love you."

He pulled the sheet up, tucking it between his shoulder and chin. "Maybe there *is* something horribly wrong with my heart, I don't know. I really don't. Hell, maybe I'm dying."

"Jack, honey. Don't talk like that. You're going to be okay," she said. "I'll sit here with you. Or do you want me to go down and get that Coke I promised you? I'll do whatever you want."

"Go on and get it. I'll be okay while you're gone."

The elevator Ann took down was crowded. Yet the passengers, absorbed in private dramas, were eerily quiet. A girl held a cluster of shiny metallic balloons that read, "Get Well Soon." As Ann watched them float against the ceiling, she wondered if she'd been cowardly in not confronting Shannon when he'd said Jack could go home.

On the first floor, an orange marker at the cafeteria's entrance warned of a slippery floor. Pots and pans clanged in the background as cooks prepared the evening meal. Ann bought two cans of soda and two cups of ice and put them in a cardboard holder to carry to the room.

As she walked back to the elevator, she realized she'd said some things that could undermine Jack's confidence in his treatment. Until she had some other options pinned down for him, she had to maintain his trust. That was a big part of the healing process. It was about all he had right now. If she agreed to spend the night in a hotel, it would signal to Jack that she was comfortable with his care, and maybe she could get a decent night's sleep too.

CHAPTER 6

Heyworth's operating room, number eleven, was double-staffed for the transplant. His patient, a middle-aged woman named Verda Travers, had the sort of intense carrot-orange hair typically seen only in children.

The first heart transplant in America had been performed at a hospital in a state near Madsen in early 1968. Over the next year, twenty-one patients underwent the procedure. The fortunate ones lived for only a few months. There were problems with kidney and liver toxicity, hypertension, racking seizures—the symptoms of organ rejection. Critics harped about heedless experimentation, about the expense, about doctors playing God.

Heyworth had diagnosed Verda Travers six months ago and put her on the waiting list for a new heart. She'd visited his office every six weeks to chat with Constance and get an update about her position on the list, always dressed in shiny black boots, black jeans, a colorful denim shirt. Heyworth talked with her each time and tried to keep her from becoming too depressed.

There were complications during Verda's transplant operation. The heart, due to arrive from Kansas City on a carefully timed schedule, was delayed because engine problems forced the airplane to land at an airport sixty miles away. This put Heyworth under pressure, because a heart, once taken from a body, has a short life. As they waited, his challenge was to stay calm while the staff in the operating room began to panic because things were not going as they should.

When the organ finally arrived, he made decisions quickly, sewing in the new heart in an intense effort to make up time. When his work was done, Heyworth's scrubs were heavy with sweat. He watched Verda pass by on the gurney as she was rolled out toward intensive care, confident she'd return to ranching and horseback riding.

In the locker room, Heyworth took a hot shower and put on fresh scrubs, his white coat. On his way back to his office, he took a detour through the doctors' lounge. This large room was filled with couches, Lazy Boy chairs, square tables cluttered with the day's newspapers.

The only person there was the heavyset Dr. Tolson, who stood at the food buffet with a half-filled paper plate in his hand.

"How's your day been?" Tolson asked in Heyworth's direction as the doctor entered.

"Pretty crazy." Heyworth grabbed a cold muffin at the far end of the buffet. "Yours?"

"A little better than usual. Certainly better than the last time we talked."

Heyworth gave him a vacant stare.

"When I came by your office to talk to you about my Medicare audit. Remember that?"

"Yeah…sure. I remember."

Heyworth walked on toward the door, his head down, eating his muffin. With the surgery over, he could think of nothing else except that he needed to get back to his office so he could call his lawyer to discuss the FBI rumor.

"Did I say something wrong?"

"No," Heyworth said, looking back.

Tolson shook his head. "You're hard to be a friend to sometimes, you know that?"

Heyworth opened the door to leave. "I'm sorry," he said, buttoning up his smock. "I've just got to go."

*   *   *

Heyworth's attorney, Hallie Echols, worked in one of the skyscrapers visible out his office window. When he told her of Dr. Eddington's rumor, Hallie questioned him about Eddington's credibility. To comfort him, she added that any FBI investigation of him would likely come out in the process of discovery and uncovering evidence, assuming it was a civil case, not a criminal one.

"Get something more solid than a rumor, David," she said with lawyerly skeptcism.

Heyworth was tired from the transplant operation, yet nervous energy surged in him as he held the phone. "Let's assume for a moment that the rumor is true, Hallie. Maybe the FBI is just beginning its investigation, and this is the first sign of it."

"David," she said. "You're too good a doctor to be worrying about this kind of crap."

"Come on, Hallie. Advise me as a friend. I want to know what I'm up against."

She had some expertise in the subject: One of her law partners handled defense work in health care fraud; the firm's clients were nationwide and included agencies like the FBI, the Drug Enforcement Agency, the IRS, even Customs.

"All right," she said in her husky voice. "The federal government has enormous resources with which to prosecute, and the FBI, in particular, is putting energy into these types of investigations. Now as to whether an FBI investigation of some sort has you as one of its targets, well, I think that's a little far-fetched, frankly."

"Why? Couldn't I be, in theory? Explain to me why not."

"David," she said, sounding exasperated by his persistence.

Heyworth's hard breaths into the phone made a rush in his earpiece.

After an awkward silence, Hallie's tone was more understanding. "Most clients caught up in these federal cases are good people who've made an error in judgment," she said. "My advice is to pay attention to what you're doing—which you always do—and you'll have nothing to worry about."

Heyworth's stomach dipped a little as he recalled a patient: the man from Utah who'd gotten mad over his bill and vowed to make trouble. What was his name? he wondered.

"You still there?" Hallie said.

His mind was reeling. A threat to him was a threat to his patients. He wondered if getting involved with the Lewis case was a prudent thing to do. "If a doctor did find himself in trouble, Hallie, how would it play out, typically?"

"This is speculation, David."

"Then speculate for a minute."

"Well, typically the Feds cast a wide net. The charges are vague. They allege any and everything."

"What exactly is any-and-everything?"

She sighed. "If, for example, you've filed false Medicare claims by mail, then that's mail fraud. If you've used the phone, that's wire fraud. They start there. Then they go after someone on the inside—nurses, secretaries, office workers—charge them with conspiracy. It scares the hell out of these people. They lean on them and turn them against you."

Heyworth heard someone out in the hall. "Hold on," he said. Constance passed by his doorway, and when her office door closed, he said to Hallie, "Okay, go ahead."

"You get the gist of what I'm saying, don't you?" Heyworth's silence told Hallie he was still fixated on the matter, so she went on, her cadence faster. "If you're lucky, the case gets caught up in the logjam at the U.S. attorney's office. But if it does go to jury, all this sounds terrible— money laundering, even racketeering can get thrown in on top of the wire and mail fraud. Makes it even tougher to persuade the jury of the client's innocence. It's an ordeal, David. A real ordeal."

"I see." Heyworth's voice was low, as if he were in a trance. What he'd heard was so over the top, so contrary to his nature that he couldn't absorb it.

"You prodded me on this, David," Hallie said, as if realizing she'd gone too far.

The conversation had run its course. After he said good-bye and hung up, his shoulders seemed heavy and his breath was short. When he felt calmer, he called Constance and she appeared in the doorway.

"Don't take what I'm about to say the wrong way," he said.

"Okay," she replied warily as she came in and sat down.

Heyworth touched his mouth, then cleared his throat. "Constance, how sound are our Medicare coding procedures?"

"Oh, Susan was one of the best clerks we ever had. I'm just sorry we had to let her go when the administration took over our billing."

"I seem to remember that the last time we did job reviews you said Susan needed more training."

"She always needed training because the Medicare codes were always changing and the insurance company's codes and forms have gotten more complex, too." Constance narrowed her eyes. "You're worried about that visit by Dr. Eddington and the FBI rumor he told you about, aren't you?"

He felt helpless. "I just don't want any problems, Constance. Have our coding procedures been sound for a long time? Ever since you've been here?"

"Don't worry," she said. "This office is run tightly. If there are mistakes, they are minor and quite innocent."

*   *   *

Heyworth left the hospital in his black Mercedes. The sun was setting on one of the summer's hottest days and he opened the window and felt the searing wind. His worry about the FBI rumor and the intrigue at the hospital made him remember an incident that happened last year.

There was a doctor he knew, though not well, a Dr. Max Smith, whom the administration had considered a nuisance. The administration planted a tape recorder in Dr. Smith's operating room. One day during an intense operation, they pulled the doctor's longtime nurse and a relatively untrained nurse was put in. This nurse happened to be a woman of color, and when little things went wrong during the surgery—instruments got misplaced, responses to commands took too long—Dr. Smith erupted, just as they knew he would. Words were said that shouldn't have been and the administration had every syllable on tape. The doctor was rebuked, made to take a class in sensitivity. The incident scarred him, wore him down, and he left the hospital several months later.

As Heyworth drove, he wondered if the FBI rumor was a tactic the hospital administration was using to try to wear him down.

When he got home, Cab pawed at him as he poured a glass of wine in the kitchen. He took a long drink just as Marge walked in. Her blouse was sweat-stained and wrinkled—she had just returned from watching Aline's tennis match, which had run over into the evening.

"Who won?" he asked.

"We did. The other girl has more raw talent, but Aline just kept hitting it back like she was a wall. It was a classic display of her grit and brains. She reminded me of you in some ways. You should've seen her. You really should have been there."

"You're not going to let go of it, are you?"

Marge was wounded by his tone. "Let go of what, David?"

"Of making me feel guilty about not being there for Aline."

She turned to the window over the sink. "You must've had a really bad day at the hospital."

"I did, now that you ask." Heyworth took another long drink, staring out the window with her. "Marge, there's a rumor at the hospital of an

FBI investigation. I might be involved in some way, though I'm not sure exactly how. A doctor came to me this afternoon and told me about it."

She put her hand on the counter top to steady herself. Her expression told Heyworth he needed to explain further.

"It was a doctor I don't know very well. It may be just a rumor."

"And if it's not?"

He was unnerved by her question, and as Marge ran water on her hands at the sink, he thought of telling her about his earlier conversation with his lawyer. But that would only alarm her, he decided. He shook his head, closed his eyes tightly, and when he looked back at her, his restraint gave way.

"There are so many rules and regulations in medicine now," he blurted. "If they want to find someone guilty of some so-called violation, the powers-that-be can nail damn near any doctor."

She dabbed her cheeks with a wet cloth. "What am I supposed to say when you tell me about something like this, David. I'm sorry, but I just don't know how to respond. I mean, how do you expect me to react?"

His shoulders drooped. "I can't keep this kind of thing bottled up in me. I needed to tell you about it whether you want to hear it or not."

"It's not that I don't want to hear about it. It's just seems so bizarre, so difficult to relate to, that I—"

The phone rang and startled both of them. Marge looked at it and said that Aline had promised she would call if she was going to be late.

Heyworth moved into the study and sat with his feet propped on the ottoman. He heard Marge's voice in the kitchen and realized it was Marge's friend, Colette, calling from the theater.

Just as Marge hung up, Aline came in the back door. He strained to hear their conversation in the kitchen and thought of how much more troubled their marriage would become if he were caught up in an FBI probe and how it would change the way Aline thought of him.

Marge and Aline broke off their talk and came into the study. Aline's damp hair was crimped into rivulets, and she wore an all-white tennis outfit. Marge sat down for a moment, and then announced she was sticky from sitting outside in the heat to watch Aline earlier in the evening and she was going to take a bath.

Aline turned on the TV and changed the channel to a station playing music videos. "Is Mother okay?" she asked during a commercial. "She went off to the bedroom kind of suddenly."

"She's just tired, I think."

"The other night I heard her talking on the phone to Colette, and she told her that she's beginning to feel okay about my leaving."

"She's working through it. She's going to miss you, and so am I."

Aline got up and walked stiff-legged to the kitchen. Heyworth wondered how much Marge had told her of their troubles. His mind drifted, cut loose from its typically-secure moorings, and he even questioned whether Marge had told Aline of some decision she'd made about their marriage that she hadn't yet told him.

Aline came back in, tossing a peach up and down with one hand.

"Mother told me you played well tonight," he said to her. "She said you reminded her of me. With your determination, I mean. Not so much your tennis."

"She's told me that before. Usually when she thinks I'm being too competitive."

"Really," he said, feeling both offended and proud. He leaned toward Aline. "Honey, listen, I'm not sure how to say this."

She turned, facing him.

"Do you resent me for not being around enough while you were growing up? You know what I mean."

"No, Daddy." She bit into her peach, her eyes still on him. "Mother does sometimes, I think. But it's not coming from me."

"When you were younger you asked me why I worked all the time."

"I don't remember that."

"We were in the living room of our old house. I remember it like it was yesterday." Heyworth leaned back. "I've just been wondering how you felt these days, that's all."

"I guess the way you are has benefited me in some ways."

"You think so," he said, sensing she was trying to make him feel better.

"I've had opportunities other kids haven't had. The summer camp and, of course, all those tennis camps and that trip I took to Europe last summer, plus my car I got even a few months before I turned sixteen, stuff like that. I know you're really busy, daddy. You've done the best you can."

"I guess you've turned out pretty good," he said, grinning painfully.

They watched another music video until a loud guitar riff was played and images flashed that were so raunchy it made them uncomfortable.

"I'm going upstairs." Aline handed him the remote control. "I need to shower and get ready for bed."

"Okay. Good night, hon."

"Good night, Daddy."

Heyworth turned off the TV and took out his diary and noted the events of his day on the lined pages. In the bedroom, the lights were still on, but Marge was asleep with an open book resting face-down under her chin. He got in bed and closed his eyes.

The next morning, Heyworth was out just after sunrise. There was a long, steep hill near his house and from his starting point which was a mailbox, he sprinted up the grade with choppy strides. The air was moist and he smelled the wet pavement and heard the far-off bark of a dog. At the hill's crest, he turned and trotted back down, and when he took off again to go up, he sprinted a bit faster and repeated this cycle until he was winded and pleasantly fatigued and clear-headed.

Back home, he stretched on the patio and then showered and dressed. When he emerged from his walk-in closet, Marge was propped up in bed, leaning back on her elbows. She'd been awake while he dressed.

"How are you?" he said.

"Didn't sleep well. Again. Not a good week for sleep." Her lips were dry, and she swallowed with effort. "I've been thinking about what you said about leaving medicine."

He sat on the bed's edge. "Marge, listen. I will not be spooked by this FBI thing, if that's what you're implying."

She lay back into her pillows. "All I'm saying is be careful. You're really important to me."

He straddled her with his knees and put his hands behind her head, and she clutched the edges of his shoulders tightly. There was a thread of connection between them for the first time in a while, and they lingered, kissing.

"I've got to go," he said as he reluctantly pushed himself up off the bed. "I'll see you tonight."

Heyworth went out the back door and headed to the hospital.

∗   ∗   ∗

Ann Lewis woke up, and it took her a moment to remember she was in a hotel room near Mercy Hospital. She'd dreamed and images lingered. A white-coated doctor high in a tree had summoned her, and she had scraped her feet against the rough bark but couldn't climb up, and as she sat looking up ripe fruit pelted the ground around her. After she thought of this, she took out her Bible and read a few verses in Matthew, but found no peace or guidance in them.

In the bathroom, she ran hot water in the tub and let it rise to her chest, her feet propped against the side. She considered that she hadn't been able to see Heyworth yesterday after he'd examined Jack. She could take her husband home to Southpointe in just a few hours if she'd just do as Shannon had recommended. This meant no arguing with Jack, no more worrying about finding another doctor for him.

She wrapped herself in two towels, plopped onto the bed and dialed Jack's room.

"You okay over there?"

"Mr. Lewis is no longer with us," Jack said, disguising his voice with a deep TV announcer's baritone. "The news was just on CNN. He passed away."

"Jack, if this is your way of coping, I don't like it one bit."

He went on, rebelliously. "Call Mr. Lewis's funeral home. He's got a big funeral coming."

She sighed into the phone.

"Well, hurry on over here," Jack said in his normal voice. "I'm anxious to get out of this hospital one way or the other."

Ann dressed, fixed her hair and put on powder, mascara, lipstick. Grover Street, the main road running through the medical center, was packed with cars and buses and pedestrians and as she crept along, the red-brick mass of the hospital loomed ahead. She went in the front entrance, past the gift shop and the wall-placard by its door that read, "Be ye kind one to another."

Up on the third floor, a throng of hospital staffers burst through the double-doors behind Ann, and a patient was whooshed past on a gurney. When the hallway quieted, she heard her name called.

"Mrs. Lewis," the nurse behind the high counter repeated. "We'll be ready to check your husband out at noon. We'll have the papers before long."

Ann nodded hypnotically at the woman as if pulled along by an undertow. She started down the hall towards Jack's room, but veered off into the open waiting area near where two boys in their late teens were sitting. One of the boys had fine sandy-brown hair that reminded her of Neal's hair when he was much younger, and she thought of calling her son to get his advice. But what could he tell her? she thought, and then she realized she had to try to talk to Dr. Heyworth again.

Before heading to the doctor's office, she checked on Jack.

"Morning there," she said as she neared his bed. "I see you're not dead after all."

"I survived without you here last night. But barely."

Ann realized he wasn't altogether kidding. "What is it?" she said, her tone demanding. "What's wrong?"

He avoided her eyes as if regretting what he'd started. "I don't want you getting all twitterpated about it. It's probably not that big of a deal."

"I don't know whether it's a big deal or not if you won't tell me what it is."

"Never mind."

"Jack. Please. I'm too tired for this. I promise to behave. Whatever."

"After you left last night, a nurse came in," he said, his eyes straight ahead. "I snapped at her a little bit because she pinched me accidentally when she took my pulse or whatever the heck she was doing to me."

"Was it that little black-headed nurse?"

He turned to Ann. "I told you I don't want you raising a fuss over it."

She bowed her head in a show of exaggerated contrition. "Finish your story."

"Anyway, this little nurse sat down on the floor and started crying and went on and on about how she didn't have time to care for all the patients and about how she had too much to do around here. I finally calmed her down."

Ann shook her head as she backed away.

"I shouldn't even have told you about it." He rolled over onto his side, facing her, yet staring blankly at the wall. Finally, he said, "Am I okay?"

"What do you mean?"

"I mean, do you think everything's okay around this hospital? You know more about all this stuff than I do."

Ann turned to the door.

"Where you going, hon?" he called after her.

"I've just got to take care of a few last-minute things before we check out."

"You promised not to say anything to anybody about that little nurse," he shouted over the sound of the door closing.

*   *   *

Heyworth came in the back door to his office suite, his surgical mask pushed down around his neck. As he passed the receptionist's desk, he saw Ann Lewis in his waiting room and waved her inside.

She walked past him to his office. A streak of sunlight washed over one side of Heyworth's desk.

Without waiting until they were seated, she told Heyworth how Shannon had recommended that Jack be sent home and treated with drugs. Heyworth untied the strings of his mask at the back of his neck as he listened, his expression grave.

Ann was red-eyed, at the ragged edge even after a night's sleep in a regular bed. "You haven't discussed my husband's case with Dr. Shannon, have you?"

Heyworth shook his head. "But there are reasons for that, as you can imagine." He knew Ann was aware of the tension between Shannon and himself because of how she'd tried to disguise the reason for his visit to Jack's room yesterday when the nurse entered. "There are questions as to the best way to treat your husband, Mrs. Lewis," he added.

Ann sat back, her eyes fixed on the doctor.

"There are many factors to consider—your husband's condition, the pros and cons of various treatments, the likelihood the treatment will improve his quality of life."

"It sounds like you think he's received proper treatment."

"Not necessarily."

Heyworth wanted to show Ann the images of Jack's heart and arteries on the X-ray box to illustrate his point, but the X-rays and CT scans weren't on his credenza. He realized Constance had stored them in the hallway knook and stood to go get them.

"Wait," Ann said.

Heyworth was held there by the trace of panic in her voice. He sat back down.

"I'm sorry," she said. "I just don't want you to get away from me today. That happened yesterday when you had that transplant surgery."

"You could've called me at home last night. Constance has my pager number."

"I didn't think of that. Last night I was confused and tired of fighting and, oh…I don't know."

Heyworth faced the sunlight. When he finally looked back at her, he paused to clear his throat. "My recommendation is for your husband to have a bypass surgery. He's going to live longer and be more comfortable."

Ann bowed her head. "All this heart surgery stuff was just coming into medicine when I was in nurses' training in the early nineteen-sixties. It was the new thing back then."

"I understand," he said. "This is not an easy decision. Your husband will have a lot to say about it, I'm sure. Perhaps you should go discuss it with him."

Ann bounced her fist thoughtfully against her chin. "Let's plan to go ahead as you see fit, Doctor. Just tell me what I need to do." Then she remembered. "What am I thinking? My husband's scheduled to check out at noon. That's less than an hour from now."

Like most doctors, Heyworth had shuffled patients in and out of the hospital to circumvent Medicare and insurance company limits on the number of days patients could be hospitalized with reimbursement. Checking Jack Lewis out might help avoid any interference from Drew Shannon or his nurses. Then, the rumor he'd heard the day before rushed in his mind. But he shook it off. "Don't worry, Mrs. Lewis. Go ahead and check out."

Ann stood up abruptly. "You don't mean you're not going to help us? That's not what you're saying, is it, Doctor?"

Constance almost clipped Ann with the edge of the door on her way in. She apologized and laid out Heyworth's bowl of tuna salad, a fork, a paper towel and a glass of water. "They're about ready down in the O.R.," Constance told him. "You need to eat your lunch early."

"How's my schedule tomorrow morning?"

"There's a hole until noon. Though I'm sure it will fill up with something."

"Schedule a bypass surgery for as early as possible." His eyes urged Constance to leave the room. "I'll give you the details later," he assured her.

The bowl of tuna and lettuce filled the center of Heyworth's desk. He leaned over it, talking to Ann. "You can take your husband to a nearby hotel. If he's okay with doing the surgery, we'll bring him back to pre-op tomorrow morning."

Ann smiled, but when she thought about the ordeal ahead, her face tightened. "Can you come by our room before he checks out of the hospital and explain to him what's going on?"

"I definitely need to discuss all this with your husband, Mrs. Lewis. I want to explain to you both what we're doing and why and the risks involved." But it wasn't wise for him to come by the room. "When you get to your hotel, call Constance and leave her your room number. I'll come there later."

Heyworth couldn't see Ann's expression, so he moved around his desk, where she stood.

"Are you okay with all this, Mrs. Lewis?"

"I know you're in a tough position," she said, her voice unsteady.

"I have my own reasons for doing this. And don't worry, I'll handle Dr. Shannon. I'll talk to him about all this later, when the time is right."

*   *   *

Ann helped Jack dress without saying much to him. She was having difficulty getting him into his bright-blue, one-piece jumpsuit, a holdover from the 1970s, when an attendant rolled in the wheelchair she'd requested.

"We're not taking that contraption home, are we?" Jack said as she finally zipped up his jumpsuit.

"It's a long walk to the front door." Ann patted the wheelchair's back, which had the hospital's logo emblazoned on it. "Rest your bones here."

"I don't plan on needing any help getting around when I get home," he said as he stood. "I sure as heck can't play golf from a wheelchair."

"We're not taking it home," she said, trying to placate him.

He sat awkwardly in the wheelchair, and it rolled backwards with his weight. The attendant didn't notice so Ann grabbed Jack's knee to stop his momentum.

"My balance is off," Jack said. "I'll be better. I've been laying down too long."

Ann handed the wheelchair off to the attendant and told Jack she was going to get the car and meet them in the driveway. She gathered a handbag and wedged a paper sack full of dirty clothes into the side of Jack's wheelchair.

On her way downstairs, she looked up at the mirrored ceiling in the elevator and thought that tomorrow she'd be back in the hospital waiting for Jack to recuperate from his surgery. If everything went right. If there were no further complications. She worried whether the hotel she'd just checked out of hours before would let them check back in as early as noon.

On the first floor, she passed oil paintings of the doctors, the gift shop, the columnar directory from which she'd gotten Heyworth's office number just days before. The glass doors at the exit parted and the air outside was steamy-hot, almost oppressive.

She drove the car out of the garage and parked it under the hospital's front portico. The cream-colored Grand Marquis blocked one of the two lanes. As the line of vehicles lengthened behind them, the attendant helped Jack into the front seat. Ann held the car door, supervising as Jack moved his limbs slowly, seemingly dragging them.

She drove down the hospital driveway, then made a U-turn to exit at the light onto Grover Street. The lunch-hour traffic was heavy with cars, supply trucks, an occasional ambulance streaming into the med center. It was only a short distance to the hotel. Ann had just a few minutes to explain the situation to Jack.

She stopped the car at a traffic light, adjusting the air-conditioner vents so as much cool air as possible blew onto him. "Hon," she said as she accelerated, "I don't know how to tell you this. But we're not going home right now after all."

Jack brushed sweat off his brow. "Then, pray tell, where are we going?"

They paused at a traffic light. The car's interior was quiet except for the rush of the air conditioner.

"We're going to stop for a while at a hotel near the hospital," she said.

"You're getting me back for telling you that I was dead when you called from the hotel this morning."

"I wish I was joking, dear."

Jack's face pinched. "What are you talking about? The doctor said I could go home, and I'm ready to go home."

"I'm ready too, Jack! As ready as you are." Ann took her eyes off the road and faced him earnestly for a second. "We're going to a hotel. A doctor is coming by there later today to see you."

"That doctor friend of yours who came to the room yesterday, by chance?"

"Yes," she said, trying to sound resolute. "He's a really good doctor. I've come to trust him. His name is Dr. Heyworth."

"I thought you said his name was Fleming."

She was shocked that Jack had remembered her little fib about the doctor's name.

"What else have you lied to me about?"

"Stop it, Jack. You know I'm not like that." She was worn down by the heat, the flurry of the morning's events, but she had yet to tell him what she most dreaded. "He says you need bypass surgery."

"Oh boy." Jack said. One edge of the gauze bandage on his forehead had worked its way loose.

"I just found out about the surgery this morning. Jack, honey, this surgery will make you well, finally, I hope. If you don't want to have it done, we won't. Just hear the doctor out. He says you'll live longer and be more comfortable with an operation."

Jack's head was pressed against the headrest. He wouldn't look at her. "I just want to go home right now. I can think about all this better at home."

"Jack. No. I'm not driving you home. You can think about it in the hotel room. You don't realize all the work I've had to do to get us to this point."

The car's interior darkened as she pulled under the hotel's covered passageway in front of the entrance. Ann got out, turning to Jack before she closed the door.

"I'm going inside to check us in and get a room key. You wait here, now, okay."

He cut his eyes at her. "Where do you think I'm going to go?"

*   *   *

Near twilight that evening, Heyworth made his way to the Lewises' hotel room. A pastel bedspread lay at the end of the bed Jack occupied. Beyond the open curtain, the adjacent medical towers loomed, their red lights pulsing to ward off low-flying aircraft.

Heyworth noticed that Jack's pallor was worse than when he'd examined him the day before and he had a nervous glint in his eye.

"How you doing, Mr. Lewis?" he said.

"As best as I can figure, my wife thinks you're an honest doctor." Jack glanced over at Ann, who leaned against the desk. "She's not so sure about the other one who saw me. But what's going on here, Doctor? Why the shuffling between the hospital and the hotel?"

"Well, Mr. Lewis, I've told your wife my judgment about how we should proceed. She's shared that with you, I'm sure."

"She has, all right. You two are a pair running me around like this."

Heyworth took Jack's CT scan out of its cardboard sheath and pulled out a small flashlight. "This is the problem area in your heart," he explained, sitting on the edge of the bed. He shined the light behind the dark negative and at the round oval that showed the left main artery and the left descending artery. "This is what needs to be repaired."

Jack looked away—the images were unclear to him—and then he turned back. "Well, what's involved?"

Heyworth smoothed the bandage on Jack's forehead. "You have several blockages in your arteries," he said, speaking slowly so Jack and Ann would have time to absorb his words. "And to fix them we're going to take a vein out of your leg, sew it back onto the blocked artery beyond the blockage and then sew the other end onto the aorta which pumps blood out of the heart. To do this, we're going to have to stop your heart. The surgery takes about four hours. You'll be in the ICU for a day, out of bed the day after and in the hospital probably four days."

Jack nodded thoughtfully, his eyes wide. Behind the doctor, Ann shuffled her feet on the carpet, hanging back.

Heyworth let his words sink in, then continued: "There's a risk of heart failure, bleeding, infections and a lengthy recovery time. There's a chance though it's a small one that something could go wrong. You need to be aware of that."

"And if I don't have the surgery?"

"You'll have a higher risk of heart troubles. Possibly serious ones."

On the bed, Jack shifted his weight onto one hip. "I reckon I'm with you," he said with a drawling emphasis that conveyed a grudging confidence.

Heyworth took out a consent form from his back pocket. "I have something for you and your wife to read."

"How much of a chance is there that something could go wrong?" Jack asked.

"Small. One or two percent." When Jack digested this and seemed satisfied, Heyworth handed over the document. "Make sure both of you understand this. Then sign it. I'll give you some time alone."

Heyworth went out and stood by a window in the hallway. Outside, a helicopter whisked past and descended suddenly onto a nearby helipad.

Minutes later, Ann opened the door, holding the signed form in both hands like it might break. "We're all set," she said.

Heyworth put his arm around her. "Tomorrow morning, bring him to the Union Street outpatient entrance at six o'clock and go straight to pre-op. If you're asked what you're doing, tell them you have a surgery scheduled with me."

He wrote his pager number on a scrap of paper. "You can reach me tonight or tomorrow morning if you need me. And tell Jack not to eat or drink anything past midnight. That's important."

After she took the number, Heyworth stepped past her towards the room but she stayed at the window, scratching her gray head. "There's something else we need to clarify, Doctor. Or at least I need to."

"What is it, Mrs. Lewis?"

"I'm almost embarrassed to ask you this—my husband's not going to get some sort of inferior treatment because of the way we're doing this? I mean he's not going to run out of bandages or blood or anything like that, is he?"

Heyworth smiled sadly. "Of course not, Mrs. Lewis."

"Another thing," she said, moving closer to him. "This surgery isn't covered by my husband's insurance, is it?"

Heyworth shook his head. "I'm the only one who's approved the procedure."

"Well, I'm wondering how we pay you."

"Can you afford to pay me?"

She pursed her lips. "We're not poor, Doctor, but we're certainly not rich either."

"My father was a country physician," he said. "He bartered with some patients. Corn, garden vegetables, cattle. One patient even built a fence around our property. Like him, I've always considered myself a businessman so I'll make you a deal. A bypass costs around thirty-three-thousand dollars. My typical fee is five-thousand dollars. This case is important to me for a number of reasons, so I'll lower my fee. Pay me thirty-thousand dollars and I'll reimburse the hospital for its costs."

She looked at him without saying anything.

Heyworth knew he'd forgive the debt if she couldn't pay. He'd recently treated a woman from Ohio who showed up in his office with a hundred dollars in her pocket. "You can pay it out over time if it'll help."

"I think we can handle that, Doctor."

As Ann walked alongside him back to the room, the frustration of the past few days welled up. "You know I haven't given up trying to get some satisfaction from the insurance company. My son knows some pretty good lawyers. I'm going to have him check into this after it's all over. In fact, I may call him tonight about it."

"Okay, Mrs. Lewis."

Jack had pulled the bedspread up over him, and he gazed vacantly at his feet.

"We were plotting against you out there," Ann said, trying to cheer him up.

Jack looked at her, then at Heyworth. His face brightened.

"Are you comfortable?" Heyworth asked.

"I thought I was going to be at home tonight. But I guess I'm as comfortable as I can be right now."

"I'll see you in the morning, bright and early."

Heyworth touched Jack one more time and packed his scans in their cardboard sheath. Ann walked him to the elevator past doorways littered with room-service trays.

"Doctor, I've been meaning to ask you something," she said as they neared the elevator. "Do you believe God looks out for us? That He guides our lives and things turn out for the best?"

"I'm certainly an optimist, Mrs. Lewis."

Heyworth stepped into the empty cabin and held out his arm to keep the door from closing. "You try to get a good night's rest. I'll see you tomorrow morning after the surgery."

*   *   *

When Heyworth left the hotel, the moon was rising full and yellow-orange like a warning sign. He headed back to the hospital: he had follow-up to finish from the day's surgeries and he also wanted to nail down arrangements for the Lewis operation. He walked down a dark interior hallway, toward the light that came from his office.

Marge was sitting in the chair nearest his door.

"Hey there," he said, surprised. He leaned against his desk, his taut arms hanging out of the too-short sleeves of his scrubs.

"Constance told me you'd probably be back." Marge wore a collarless plum-colored jacket with silver studs on it. Her hair was brushed back straight and full. "She knows you pretty well, I'd say."

Marge's gaze drifted to the bookshelves. She hadn't visited his office since the annual staff Christmas party three years ago; to her, it was a symbol of what so often came between them. She went on looking at the spines of the books as if she'd never seen them before.

He waved one hand across her vision to get her attention. "What's up with you?" he said, waiting for her to divulge the reason for her visit.

"I just told the staff manager at the theater that I'm quitting. Effective tomorrow. One of the benefits of being a volunteer is that you can quit on short notice and not feel guilty."

He rubbed his head. His steel-gray hair was matted from wearing his surgical cap for hours on end. "You haven't done this hastily, have you? You've been under a lot of stress this week. We both have."

"I'm feeling stifled at the theater. I'm spending too much time doing things that really don't interest me. Right now, I just want to take that hiking trip. I'm going to Peru, I've decided."

"You are?" he said, sensing her determination.

"I want to sleep in a tent for a week, or maybe even a month. I need to stretch myself."

He rubbed his eye, his other eye fixed on her, hoping she'd say she could always go back to her volunteer work, looking for any sign that she wasn't prepared to totally discard their old life together. "Then what are you going to do? After you hike and sleep in a tent."

"I don't know, David. I don't have it all figured out yet. Hopefully, I'll grow and find out about myself." She tucked her jaw into her shoulder and moved it back and forth across the padding of her jacket, scratching her chin. "It's a little bewildering right now, but my life is shifting," she said, avoiding his gaze. "I can feel it."

"I see," he said.

She still wouldn't look at him. Heyworth spotted Jack Lewis's file on his desk. While thinking of it, he stuffed the file into his briefcase near his feet. Caught up in his thoughts about the Lewis case, he opened his drawer—he wanted Louisa for the Lewis surgery—but couldn't find the staffing schedule. He phoned Constance, but she didn't answer his call at her house so he left a message, making sure everything was set on her end for the surgery and telling her to call him if there was anything amiss.

"What was that all about?" Marge asked when he hung up.

He wondered if he should tell Marge about the Lewis case. His lip was sweaty—the office was slowly warming because the building's air-conditioning system was shut off by computer at seven o'clock each evening, even in the dead of late-summer. "A woman came to see me a few days ago. She didn't think her husband was being treated properly. I've examined him." He hesitated, twisting his neck to work out the tension. "The doctor on the case is Drew Shannon."

"So you're working with him on this," she said, knowing the answer.

"Actually, I'm going around him." He leaned back, his arms propped behind his neck. "It may cause trouble around here in the long run, I admit."

"David, why would you do this? Just last night you told me about an FBI investigation. And now you're doing something dicey like this. Why don't you just be *still* for a while?"

"The same reason you can't be still."

"What do you mean by that?"

"Marge, I don't think the patient's been provided the right treatment."

"How serious is this? Is the patient's life at stake?"

"It could be. But my integrity is at stake, I know that."

She frowned and looked out the window.

"Marge, try to understand," he said. "I've told you things will be different in time. My life is shifting, too."

"We need to make a shift together for once, David. It's getting late for us."

He pressed forward against the edge of his desk. "I have to get through this case. It's important to me."

"Then what? What happens after this case? It never seems to end with you, David. You get in deeper and deeper."

"I don't know happens after this. Maybe this foretells the end of my practice. But, like you and your situation, I don't have it all figured out and, right now, I can't focus on that."

Marge grabbed her purse and slung it over her shoulder. "I'm going home," she said. "I've had a long, stressful day. We can talk more later if you want to."

Heyworth dragged a stack of files off his desk as he moved toward her, but Marge was already in the hall. He called after her and from the dark of the corridor, and she answered, "I'll see you at home," and then the outer door of his office suite closed firmly.

He grabbed his briefcase. On his way out, his pager buzzed. It was Constance. Over the din of her disabled son's crying, she told him she and Laney had made the necessary arrangements for tomorrow's early surgery on Jack Lewis.

He drove home fast. It was nearing nine o'clock. As he was getting out of the car, Aline pulled into the driveway. Dashing ahead of him, she told him she was going out with friends and had come home just to change.

Marge was sitting at the kitchen bar, flipping through a gardening catalog. Heyworth stroked Cab while Aline talked about the movie she was going to later that night and what time she'd be home.

Opening the refrigerator, Aline told Heyworth, "Mom's going to drive me to school next week."

"Aline and I talked about it earlier," Marge said. "I can rent a car there and drive back."

Marge walked out to the patio to tend to her rosebushes. Aline sipped a Coke and looked at Heyworth.

"Do you want that?" he asked.

"What?"

"Your mother to go with you."

Aline shrugged and walked out, her mouth full, still drinking.

Heyworth went into the study. Through the blinds he saw Marge in the backyard holding a hose over the brilliant pink blooms and hoped she'd come in to talk. He watched some news, then pulled Jack's file out of his briefcase and studied it, trying to imprint on his mind the task that awaited him during tomorrow's operation.

By this time, Marge was lying down in the bedroom. She'd avoided him by coming in through the French doors off the patio. As he stretched out next to her, she turned onto her side away from him. He scooted over and curled his body around her, cupping her like a shell, his chin nestled into the soft part of her shoulder.

"Everything's moving so quickly, it seems." Marge's voice was drained of the confidence it held earlier. "I want to go with Aline. But I know it would be better if I didn't."

"Maybe you should go with her."

"I shouldn't. She didn't really ask me to go. I forced the issue earlier today. What was she going to say?"

From behind, Heyworth pulled Marge close and felt her breaths. She was strong, he knew, and he admired her for taking charge of her life.

"I'm a little scared," she said.

"About what?"

She drew her knees up tighter towards her stomach. "I've quit the theater. My daughter's leaving home. That was an unsettling conversation we had in your office. One of several lately. I don't know where our marriage is going. And I don't know where I'm going. It's all the unknowns that frighten me."

"Me, too." He kissed her cheek and thought of all that had happened the last few days, and all that still faced him. "Let's just try to hang in there," he said finally.

*   *   *

Heyworth awakened an hour early, but instead of going for his run he thrashed around in bed, fading in and out of sleep.

He got up, careful not to wake Marge, and took a shower and dressed in his scrubs. As he clipped his pager to his pocket in the kitchen, he realized Jack Lewis was on his way into pre-op at the hospital.

Heyworth re-entered the bedroom to say good-bye to Marge. She met him near the dresser, and they reached for each other at the same time.

"That surgery you told me about last night," she said as she clung loosely to him. "It's today, isn't it?"

"Yes."

She pushed him back to see his face. "Damn you, David," she said with mock disgust. "You're difficult, you know it."

"I can be...sometimes."

"I just can't offer you much support," she said, dropping her head. "I wish I had it in me right now."

They walked to the kitchen, holding hands, then to the back door. He gave Marge a quick kiss. Before he got into his car, he turned and saw her white feet against the gray concrete of the top doorstep.

"Call me later," she said. "Please."

"Don't worry now. Everything's going to be okay."

CHAPTER 7

On the Day Posting Board outside the surgical suites, the initials "CAB" were scrawled in black grease pencil in the seven-thirty a.m. time slot for operating room eleven. This was a sign the scheduling coordinators had not noticed anything unusual about Jack Lewis's readmittance to the hospital.

Inside the operating room, Jack lay under the three big round lights. The anesthesiologist had put him under. Now the circulating nurse slathered his chest and body with betadine, a sticky, brown disinfectant. Clustered around him were computer screens, gauges, dials and clocks—each measuring some essential function, including the heart-lung machine.

Heyworth strode through the double-doors. As he fitted on the eye-frames that held his surgical loops, Laney gave him some news: When Jack Lewis entered the O.R., he'd had chest pains even after getting nitroglycerine to lower his blood pressure and relieve the pain.

Laney and the nurses continued prepping and draping the body, readying the pump lines to be set into Jack's chest for bypass and cardioplegia and suction. Heyworth checked Jack's vital signs on the screen over the operating table: His cardiac enzymes were elevated and the green ribbon showing his heart waves was irregular. He consulted the cinefilm of the heart to see one last time where Jack's blockages were and what he had to do to fix them. Then he went back out to wash up.

He scrubbed his hands and arms, fumbling with the sponge and dropping it. He had jitters like he hadn't had since he'd performed a risky and innovative thoraco procedure on a patient last year.

Louisa appeared to tell him that Ann Lewis had followed her husband as he was being rolled toward the operating room and that she'd had to stop Ann because in her anxiety she'd passed the bold red line beyond which all personnel had to be dressed in sterile scrubs, caps and foot covers.

Louisa helped him dry his hands and arms and get into his gown and gloves. He cut through Jack's chest with a sternal saw and cauterized the bleeders. With a retractor, he opened the chest to get at the heart and the great vessels.

Meanwhile, Laney was cutting into the thick of Jack's thigh. She extracted the saphenous vein, which was to be grafted onto the heart later, while Heyworth harvested the internal mammary artery. When they both finished, the leg vein was placed in a metal bowl of saline solution and the artery Heyworth had loosened was ready to be repositioned.

Jack Lewis's vital signs seemed stable and Heyworth told Louisa to turn on some classical music. Laney and the nurses began a casual banter about the rigors of the August heat, even though the room temperature was at sixty degrees to keep the patient cool and the nurse nearest the supply closet had wrapped himself in a sterile white blanket.

Heyworth pared away the thin tissue surrounding the heart. The field of surgery inside Jack's chest was a jumble: white bandages, silver instruments, green sterile dressings soaked with blood; yet the doctor saw order. He dissected the aorta and the pulmonary artery and put on a cross clamp.

The next step was cannulation, draining the body of blood, and then stopping the heart. When Heyworth and Laney had everything set, they unclamped the venus line and began bypass. The clear tubes running between Jack's chest and the heart-lung machine filled with blood as the machine took over Jack's breath and pulse. His heart was stopped.

Now, every minute counted. The less time spent on bypass, the better. A bypass that took more than two hours could create complications because the patient was essentially in a state of controlled shock.

The pace of their work quickened and the tone in the room grew tense. Heyworth propped up the heart for better access. Behind him, the perfusionist working the heart-lung machine called out the heart's temperature, which eventually dropped to ten degrees Celsius, and the amount of time that had elapsed since she'd last administered cardioplegia. Heyworth honed in on the left main artery. He used blades, forceps, bulldog clamps, forward-and-reverse scissors and tiny curved needles with silk thread. As he worked, the anesthesiologist at the head of the operating table told him the amount of medicine—more than usual—that was needed to elevate Jack's blood pressure.

On the monitor above, Heyworth could see that Jack's arterial blood pressure was low. He began grafting the leg vein above and below the blockages in his arteries, putting the vein in upside down so the valves inside the leg vein would not interfere with the flow of blood.

When this was done, he focused on the next blockage, working through the surgery step-by-step, his hand moving methodically as he sewed and cut. Finally he looked up, nearly overcome by the heat underneath his gown, and flexed his hands open and shut to relieve the cramps in his fingers.

Both bypass grafts were complete. He removed the some bandages and watched as the body temperature rose on the monitor.

The next step was to get Jack's heart beating again, to bring him off bypass, but Heyworth knew something was wrong with the first irregular beats of Jack's heart—the organ began to swell and look expanded from internal pressure. The doctor had scaled the mountain, but hadn't quite gotten over the top. He couldn't get Jack's heart to work. Now he had to start over at the beginning and make another run at weaning Jack off bypass.

To stimulate the heart, he tried drugs first—norepinephrine, dopamine, dobutamine—calling out the commands to the anesthesiologist. All eyes were on the overhead monitors to see if the drugs worked. After several minutes, it was obvious they hadn't. Heyworth had to stop Jack's heart again, and then try assist devices.

The heart-lung machine once more took over, and Jack's heart was again still as if stunned. Heyworth worked through his surgical logic, trying to get over the mountain. He had encountered situations before where patients didn't immediately respond when taken off bypass, a few other cases when they never responded. His skin prickled as the consequences of Jack Lewis dying on this operating table flashed through his mind.

He tried a pacing line to gently shock the heart, but there was no response. Then he put a balloon pump in Jack's chest to take the workload off the left ventricle. Heyworth compared the time on the wall clock to his own internal clock, which told him how long the patient had been on bypass and how he was doing. Jack had been on bypass for almost two hours. Heyworth pondered his next step if the balloon pump didn't work.

He studied the monitors, the puzzlement in his eyes shielded by his surgical loops, and considered calling in Dr. Shannon to advise him as Jack's cardiologist—he was not too proud to do that if it might help.

But then Jack's heart began to shrink to a more normal size. Heyworth decided to warm his body, try to wean him off bypass again and get his heart back up.

He called out the commands to the perfusionist, who in turn shouted out the critical readings to him, back and forth, and the line monitoring Jack's blood pressure moved in the right direction. With the loosening of the clamp on the venus line, Jack's heart started to beat with a regular, forceful rhythm and his lungs pitched underneath his sternum.

When the body was warmed, Heyworth cauterized the remaining bleeders, pinned the sternum together with wires as thick as kite string and sutured the surface wound.

He stepped back, took off his surgical telescopes and gloves, mopped his forehead and stared at the floor, exhausted and relieved. After he'd gathered himself, he walked through several sets of double-doors, to the desk in the intensive-care wing. He asked the nurse there to page Ann Lewis.

Heyworth leaned against the high counter listening to the nurse's voice over the intercom. The double-door behind him opened, and Drew Shannon came through, walking full stride.

Heyworth's throat tightened. Was Shannon there now for a reason or was it just a coincidence? Given the circumstances, he should've gone to the ICU waiting room to see Ann Lewis rather than have her paged.

"That Quality Assurance citation you asked me about a few days ago," Shannon said over his shoulder as he passed by. "It was a mistake. Don't worry about it."

Heyworth nodded and watched Shannon turn the corner. Now was not the time to broach the subject of Jack Lewis's treatment.

As he stood there, Ann Lewis walked through the double-doors that led from the waiting room. Her face was drawn and expectant.

"There were some complications during the surgery," Heyworth said.

"What kind?" Her voice was calm since she'd already endured one emergency with Jack that morning.

"He had a tough time. It was worse than I expected. We're going to have to watch him. But I believe he's going to be fine."

Ann looked at Heyworth, her lips pinched. When she smiled faintly, Heyworth finally gave himself over to a grin that came from deep within him.

"He'll be in the recovery room for a while, but you can see him soon," he said.

Ann put her arms on Heyworth's shoulder in a sideways embrace and as he bent to hug her, he saw Drew Shannon coming back around the corner. He was headed right for them.

Heyworth put his arm firmly behind Ann's back. "Why don't you go get yourself something to eat, and take a little rest," he said, glancing back in Shannon's direction as he guided her. "I'll come see you in a little while."

When she was gone, Heyworth circled around the back way to his operating room to see when Jack Lewis would be coming out.

*   *   *

The morning after Jack Lewis's operation, Heyworth went to see him in intensive care just before lunch. In a rare moment, Ann wasn't there—she'd driven out to Southpointe for clean clothes and to check on their house since she and Jack had been away longer than they'd expected. The doctor checked Jack's vital signs and his chest wound to make sure it wasn't too red or swollen.

Jack looked down the length of his body as Heyworth worked. "I guess I was sicker than I thought, wasn't I, Doctor?"

"I've seen sicker."

"I read in a newsmagazine a few days ago that in Canada there's an eighteen-week wait for a bypass operation," Jack said. "I've had a lot of time to read since I've been here. You pick up all kinds of information. My wife's read everything in sight."

"I understand," Heyworth said.

"When do you figure I can get out the golf clubs again?"

"Six to eight weeks I'd give it. We're going to watch you." Heyworth pressed the long, stitched scar on Jack's sternum. "Are you tender here? Does that hurt any?"

"Not really," Jack said. "I know I was a lot of trouble down in the operating room. You really loaded yourself up when you took me on, didn't you, Doc?"

Heyworth looked up at him. "Well, you're doing pretty good now, I see."

"I'll brag about you since my wife isn't here. I'm glad she found you."

Heyworth slipped his stethoscope into his pocket. "Okay, Mr. Lewis. You're doing just fine." He gave a nodding smile that said "you're welcome" as he left the room.

That day as Heyworth made his rounds, he didn't see Drew Shannon. Later, Heyworth set out to find him so he could tell him he'd operated on Jack Lewis before Shannon found out on his own. But when Heyworth saw Dr. Tolson in the hall, he mentioned that Shannon had left for a few days on a business trip to the state capital.

Meanwhile, at Heyworth's request, Constance cleared his schedule for part of the following day—it was to be the first weekday he hadn't done a morning surgery in almost a year.

That night, Heyworth's house was filled with the sounds of a life being reshuffled—suitcases were zipped, boxes were finally taped shut, footsteps pattered up and down the carpeted staircase that led from Aline's bedroom to the back door.

The next morning was sultry and sticky. The rear of Aline's teal-green sports car was crammed with her luggage and boxes, a pillow, blanket and sheets, a computer, her cache of a half-dozen tennis racquets. While Aline squeezed her stereo in the front passenger seat, Heyworth gently pressed down the contents of the trunk before he slammed it shut.

Marge watched from inside, at a window in the utility room. She'd decided it wasn't a good idea to drive Aline after all. Yesterday, she'd helped Aline do last-minute packing, and this morning she'd gotten up early to cook a pancake breakfast. But now she hung back, standing near Cab, who lay across an air-conditioning vent.

When Heyworth and Aline entered the kitchen, Marge handed each of them a glass of ice water. Aline's cheeks were flushed from the moist heat, and she gulped her water down. Marge went to her as she finished and hugged her, creasing Aline's sweaty shirt.

"I'm going to say good-bye here." Marge's voice was firm as if she'd rehearsed her words. Yet her eyes looked frail. "I'm proud of you."

"I'll be fine," Aline said.

"Call me if you forgot anything." Marge slid her hands down Aline's arms and held her fingertips. "You're only a four-hour drive away."

"I'll be coming home fairly often, I'm sure."

Aline bent over and rubbed Cab's head and said, "Good-bye, doggy-dog."

Pretty soon, Marge walked off and left him and Aline alone at the back door.

Aline went out quickly, and Heyworth followed her through the garage. Before she got in her car, he hugged her, his arms tight around her back.

"I love you," he said.

"Love you too. Take care of Mama now."

"Do you wish she was going with you today?"

"It's going to be better on all three of us if she doesn't go. Take good care of her, will you?"

"Now don't worry. You just study hard and have fun."

Aline got in the car and rolled down her window.

"Your mother said she set up an account for you at a bank near your campus," he said.

"Yeah," she said as she put on her black-framed sunglasses. "I'll call later tonight when I get settled."

He walked beside the slowly-moving car. "You know where you're going on the campus once you get there? I mean to which dorm and all." He held up his hand urgently, trotted back to the garage, and came out clutching a red cloth that he wiped in circles over the car's dry windshield like a gas-station attendant.

"Thank you, Dad," Aline said, smiling. She rolled her window up and Heyworth barely saw her through the reflection on the glass. He waved the red towel, flopping it limply, as the car rounded the corner.

Marge sat on the tall stool at the counter in the kitchen, facing the back window. Near her was the vase of antherium and a single bird of paradise that Heyworth had ordered for her yesterday morning.

"You did pretty good with all this," he said as he came in. "Better than me in some ways."

"I got weaker as the morning wore on. Let's just not talk about it too much."

As she sipped her coffee, Heyworth watched her. "Maybe we should go see Vanessa Stoy again. Now is probably a good time for another dose of counseling."

"Maybe," she replied, sounding as if she didn't really mean it. "I want to go on this hiking expedition to Peru. I'll be gone about eight weeks."

He was surprised she'd brought it up so soon after Aline's leaving. "Your going away alone for almost two months is not going to help our relationship."

"It might. You never know," she said. "I need this trip and I can pull it together quickly. I've contacted some outfitters."

"I hate for you to leave in the wake of all that's happened this week."

"It's just a little time away, David."

He looked at her, his brow furrowed. He felt vulnerable with Aline gone and with the FBI rumor hanging over him.

"You told me that if you left medicine it would be a step toward your liberation. Didn't you say that?" She waited until he nodded yes. "Well, I feel like this trip is a step toward good things for me."

He realized he wasn't going to sway her, because the trip represented something larger that she was striving toward. "Okay," he said, nodding.

He expected her to touch him on the arm or embrace him. But she stood up and went out on the patio, carrying the morning newspaper and the rosebush clippers.

Heyworth left the kitchen and went to shower. He sat on a ledge of the stall, the hot water on his shoulders, his head against the side wall.

Would things be better when Marge came back? he wondered. If they were to be together, they would have to make changes.

As he dressed in his scrubs, his pager buzzed. When he called Constance back, he learned Ann Lewis was upset because one of the late-shift nurses had suggested it was time for Jack to be released from the hospital.

"Marge," he called out as he came through the foyer. He heard her reply but couldn't place her. "Where are you?"

She was upstairs in the bedroom that adjoined Aline's, surveying it, her hand on her chin. "The space doesn't feel as empty as I imagined it would when Aline left," she said, peeling back the heavy curtain. "It might work for a studio for me to paint in. The light is pretty good."

"It is nice up here," he said, encouraging her upbeat mood.

"Maybe I could use both rooms. Aline said she wouldn't mind if we moved her to a bedroom downstairs." She looked skeptically at the grass-cloth wallpaper, then at the gray carpet. "But I'm not sure the room's right. It's certainly not very inspiring or artsy."

"You can dress the space up," he said. "You're especially good at that. We could even knock down a wall to open it up."

"Oh, I don't know what I'm doing up here. Aline just left, but something compelled me."

Heyworth's pager went off again. Marge's gave him a what's-new look and turned to the window.

"I need to get going," he said. "We'll figure it out. I'll get home early if I can."

*   *   *

Heyworth talked to Constance on his car phone about the schedule for his afternoon surgery. When he got to the hospital, Laney was waiting for him as he'd requested just outside the door to Jack Lewis's room on the third floor. While she briefed Heyworth on Jack's condition, Ann came out into the hall.

"Doctor," she said, her face tense with worry. "One of the night-shift nurses went so far with the hints about our leaving the hospital that she asked us where we'd parked our car!"

"Yes. I know about it, Mrs. Lewis."

"After all we've been through."

When Heyworth patted Ann's arm, her expression relaxed.

Inside the room, he checked the scar on Jack's sternum and his vital signs, which were strong. Jack's face was a rosy, healthier hue.

"You can't go home today, Mr. Lewis, but tomorrow we'll see," Heyworth told him.

"My wife doesn't think it's time, but I do," Jack said. "Even though my leg hurts a little."

"That's not unusual. We took a pretty big vein out of there to fix your heart. But you're progressing nicely with no complications."

"Good," Jack grunted.

"I heard you were in the funeral-home business," Heyworth said, making conversation, enjoying the warmth of contact with his patient. "My father once owned a granary and the funeral home in the little town I grew up in. But he finally sold the funeral home because it made his patients nervous knowing he was in the undertaking business."

Jack's face reddened as he laughed. Heyworth saw Ann nervously watching her husband.

"You two don't worry about a thing," the Doctor said.

Two days later, Heyworth gave his okay. Jack Lewis checked out of Mercy Hospital, and Ann drove him home.

CHAPTER 8

A week later, Marge left for Peru. Heyworth offered to drive her to the airport, but because he'd missed a half-day's surgeries to see Aline off, Marge arranged for her friend Colette to take her.

In the days leading up to her departure, Marge didn't tell Heyworth many details about her trip. But along with the beeper number for Frank, the yardman and handyman, she gave him a copy of her itinerary, which laid out her brief time in Lima and then each day in the mountains near Cuzco, the Peruvian jungle, then down into the upper Amazon.

There was a cool fog that morning, unusual for early September. Heyworth waited as Marge called the airline to make sure the flight wasn't delayed. It was on time and he decided to go on to the hospital because feared being home alone after she left.

She hugged him at the back door. "Eight weeks is not that long," she said.

"I'll be waiting for you."

"This is going to be good for me." She disguised her excitement with a little joke. "At least I'll have a nice tan," she said.

He nodded, tight-lipped. "You know," he said, "I've come through something that's deeply affected me. Hopefully, things will be better here when you get back. Look forward to that, okay?"

He mustered a smile and picked up his briefcase and his plastic bowl filled with tuna salad that she'd made for him one last time before leaving. As he walked to his car, there was an unfamiliar jittery quaking in his gut.

*   *   *

After Marge left on Friday, Heyworth spent all day Saturday and also Sunday afternoon at the hospital, trying to shake his uneasy feeling by losing himself in his work. Sunday night, he was at home working on his paper. By Monday and Tuesday, he'd settled into his routine of an early-morning run, surgeries and rounds to see his patients, tuna lunches in his office.

On Wednesday, after a bypass surgery, Heyworth found one of the bright-yellow notes on his desk that Constance occasionally left there to draw his attention to an important matter. Underneath it was a page with an FBI logo. He saw the words Press Release, and his adrenaline surged as he read:

The U.S. Attorney General announced today that more than 500 federal law enforcement officers made arrests in over 30 cities and towns as part of "Operation Patient Shield." This is one of the most widespread criminal fraud investigations of the health care industry ever carried out. Agents arrested more than 100 health care providers—including 80 doctors.

Health care fraud is a serious crime that cheats the government and private industry, taking vast numbers of dollars from the pockets of Americans who pay taxes.

This investigation is one of many being pursued to preserve the quality and integrity of our health care system. Today's actions are the first phase of investigations of those people who fraudulently siphon money from the health care system without regard to others.

Nothing had happened to him, Heyworth thought. All this law enforcement had come down on somebody somewhere, yet he was untouched by it.

Constance came in. "I got that off the Internet," she said as she hovered over him.

Heyworth's eyes turned back to the press release, and his relief turned to ire as he considered its assumptions about doctors, the sanctimony and naked power behind it. Sure, there were unscrupulous doctors out there, but there was unethical behavior in every profession. Further law enforcement dragnets were sure to come with bureaucratic technicalities to snare the unwary.

As he crumpled the press release, Constance handed him another sheet of paper. "Looks like the other shoe has dropped on the Lewis case."

Heyworth read the short memo, which stated he would no longer have exclusive use of operating room eleven. This would further cut into his income, and compromise his ability to use his operating room as a laboratory to innovate.

He rose from his desk, stuffing the memo and the wadded-up FBI press release into his pocket.

Constance stepped out of his way. "Where you off to?"

"I'm going at this head on."

At the hospital's executive suites, Heyworth barged into Shannon's office. Shannon was sitting at the conference table with two men. When he saw Heyworth, he stood and introduced the men to him. They were lawyers for the hospital. Shannon gave the two men a nod to signal that their business was finished.

As they left, Shannon walked over to the window, his head bowed as if his meeting with the lawyers preoccupied him. Heyworth pulled out the memo and laid it on the lacquered table.

"What's the thinking behind this?" he said.

"You know my philosophy," Shannon said, after glancing at the page. "We're moving toward sharing resources more evenly. That includes your operating room."

Heyworth shook his head, his arms folded tight across his white smock. "I don't like it. I've had this operating room for almost twelve years now."

"Things change. We have to adapt. All of us."

"I've been expecting something like this. Some retribution for the Lewis case."

"Is that what you think this is? It's completely unrelated, as a matter of fact. But I have been meaning to talk to you about that case ever since I got back. The way you handled it does present a problem and you knew it would when you got involved."

"The patient's wife came to me with concerns about her husband's treatment."

"You should've talked to me about her concerns."

"Not under the circumstances."

"What circumstances, Doctor?"

"Because of what I know about you, Drew. Because of the direction things are headed at this hospital."

"That patient almost died in the operating room."

"The patient had chest pains when he came in that morning. It was the day after you dismissed him. I saw the release you signed. I handled the patient as I saw fit."

Shannon's face got red, and as he came closer, he straightened his wire glasses. "My diagnosis on that patient was sound."

"It wasn't." Heyworth stared until Shannon backed away. "But I'll never convince you otherwise."

"The staff here knows what you did," Shannon said. "Your actions were disrespectful and reckless."

"My intent was to help the patient."

"Goddamn your intentions!" Shannon snatched up the memo and waved it. "These cutbacks on your operating room privileges. They've been in the works for weeks now, even months. This should be the least of your worries."

"Don't threaten me."

Shannon paced, his hands clasped behind him. "This hospital can't condone its doctors going around other doctors to treat patients. It doesn't matter whether it's my patient or any other doctor's patient."

"Mr. Lewis needed the treatment I gave him. What I did was proper. More than that, it was right."

"It was proper for your wallet," Shannon replied, his mouth turned down.

Heyworth unfolded the wadded FBI press release and pointed at it. "Someone here spread a rumor that I was under investigation by the FBI."

Shannon glared at the page. Hours before he'd heard the news about the FBI's Operation Patient Shield when Dr. Harrelson was apprehended at the outside lab he owned. "I can't control rumors around here," he said. "Surely, you don't expect that."

"No. But such rumors are another means to wear people down. The administration at this hospital is not above using this sort of thing."

Shannon tensed as if to strike Heyworth. "You treated a patient without proper referral, and you didn't get authorization for surgery. You've misused hospital resources."

Heyworth looked hard at Shannon, yet his mind was ahead of the moment, beyond this particular argument. "You'll have my letter of resignation within the week," he said.

When Heyworth got back to his desk, he took off his smock and sat down. He had been moving toward that decision for months, years even, but he hadn't imagined the end would unfold that way. Nevertheless, his mind settled quickly and he felt calm.

He wanted to talk to Marge, to hear comforting words he knew she'd convey. But according to her itinerary she was hiking in the mountains and unreachable by phone. Unless he sent her an emergency message, he wouldn't be able to communicate with her until she returned to her hotel in Lima in almost six weeks.

He considered calling his father out in San Belladro but Heyworth didn't want to broach such a weighty matter over the phone, especially since he hadn't spoken with Lloyd for several weeks.

Constance stood in his doorway. Her concern over what had happened with Shannon had kept her at the office late.

"Come in," Heyworth said. "How's your son's new school program?"

"He's made progress. The pace of the program fits him better. He's a sensitive boy. Anyway, how are things with you?"

He leaned back, his hands clasped behind his head. "I've decided to leave my practice, Constance. It's time to move on."

She sank down in the chair, shock registering on her face. Heyworth swiveled away from her, staring out at the sky and the tree line and the distant skyscrapers. Constance looked out, too, and after a moment they made eye contact through their reflections on the windowpane.

"What exactly did you tell Dr. Shannon?" Constance said. "What did you two talk about?"

"The Lewis case. And some other matters."

"I knew you were upset when you left the office, but I didn't expect this." She stared down into the middle of his desk. "I sensed you were headed in this direction. But not now. Not so abruptly."

"I know. When I got up this morning, I didn't think my day would end like this."

As Heyworth took one of the pills he kept in drawer for upset stomach, Constance stood up and began dabbing her moist eyes with a knuckle. Heyworth sat still for a moment and then came around to the front of his desk so the two of them were at arm's length.

"What did Shannon say when you told him you were quitting?"

"It doesn't matter what he said, or will say. He's not really the issue here."

"I suppose you're right."

"My mind and emotions have been moving toward this decision for some time. It was inevitable. You said earlier you sensed that."

She ran her fingers through her thick black hair until a clump of it stood up. A look of hesitant acceptance crossed her face.

"I probably should've given you more warning," he said, "considering all that we've been through together. There have been some other things happening in my life that led me to this decision. Things you might not know about. Problems with my marriage, and changes with Aline leaving."

"I understand," she said. "Don't worry about me. I'll be okay with all this."

"We can talk about it some more tomorrow if you want to. We'll need to think about how to handle the staff, and also how to take care of the patients we have in the works."

"I know," she replied as she left his office. "I'll have some recommendations ready for you."

*   *   *

Heyworth immediately turned on all the lights at home and went to the phone to call Aline. But there was no answser so he logged onto his computer and started a letter to her.

Dear Aline,

I called but missed you. Hope your first semester is going well so far. I think about you everyday. I know that when you were deciding where to go to college, you considered Madsen College. I think it was your mother's idea. At the time, I didn't think much of this because the school is here, but maybe I should have encouraged you to stay closer to home, not that it would have mattered much in your decision. One thing I've realized lately is how much you are your own person. And how much I miss you.

I am going to see your grandfather in San Belladro this weekend. Your campus is sort of on the way there (as luck would have it). I know we usually don't go to Grandpa's until Thanksgiving but it would mean a lot to me if you would come. I have some news I want to share with you.

Let me know.
Love, Dad

*   *   *

In the days that followed, Heyworth heard whisperings in the hospital's hallways, and in the locker room off the surgical suites about his confrontation with Shannon.

When anyone asked him why he was leaving, he said his affiliation with the hospital had been rewarding and he would miss medicine, but it was time for a change. But most people at the hospital took the news about Heyworth as just another instance of a doctor in late middle-age retiring early. And with the rumor mill working overtime about the possible indictment of Dr. Harrelson, there was less attention left for Heyworth.

Heyworth's daily routine at the hospital was not much changed: He was busy with his backlog of patients and also the new doctor with whom he was to share his operating room had not yet settled in. But by the next week his work load had already tapered off a bit, and the following week his surgery schedule was down to just three patients.

By the end of the fourth week, he and Constance had wrapped up the business affairs of his practice and placed his staff members with other doctors. Though Constance had another job offer, she'd decided to take a break from medicine to spend more time with her son. On one of Heyworth's last days, when he heard a clerk mention a going-away party for him, he pulled Constance aside and told her he didn't want to be eulogized.

He boxed up his editions of The Annals of Thoracic Surgery, his Osler's Histories and the textbook he'd written, the small, square wooden boxes that held his surgical telescopes, his plaques and all the sentimental trappings of his office: Among them the yellowed pillow his mother had sewn for him, the book-end busts ofdoctors from antiquity that he took home on his last day and placed on the shelves of his study.

For the first time since his summers as a teenager, Heyworth had no place to go, nowhere to be. He roamed his house sock-footed and noticed details like the morning sunlight moving across the floor in the breakfast nook, the exact time the mailman came, the programmed triggering of the sprinkler system near sunset.

In the early mornings, he did his sprints on the hill near his house, and some afternoons he drove north and hiked with the dog in the woods. He grew a beard of gray stubble like a professor's. Boxes of books, medical magazines and papers cluttered his study. He became better acquainted with Frank, Marge's handyman, who came by twice a week to tend to the yard and the swimming pool.

Yet during these days, he kept his mind on medicine, working on his paper, "Twelve-year Operative Experience with 307 Thoracic Aortic Aneurysm Surgeries," and when he buried himself in the writing he forgot his fear of losing connection with what he'd been all his life. But again and again, he dreamed that a cloth sack was being pulled down over his head, and he'd wake up alone in bed, his chest and shoulders aching with loss.

One day, among the bills and catalogues and political solicitations in his mailbox, he found an envelope with his name scrawled crookedly on it as if the writer had slightly misjudged the angle of the page. On the back was the return address, 12 Tranquil Glen, Southpointe.

He sometimes got letters from patients—notes of appreciation, updates, holiday greetings. Constance always put them on top of the pile of mail for him because she knew he liked getting them. He opened the letter:

Dear Dr. Heyworth,

I'm sure you're curious about Jack. Though he was a bit depressed when he first came home and he sometimes complains of leg pains, he seems fully recovered from his heart troubles. Every time I ask him how he's doing, he says he's upright and taking nourishment. And then he grins. He's back to playing golf and he's even

*helping me some with the yard work. I thank the Lord for each day
we have together.*

*A friend who runs in medical circles out here told me you left the
hospital. I'm sorry to hear that. The hospital sent me a questionnaire
after we got home asking if we would recommend their services to
others and I wrote them to say I'd never send a friend or relative
there except to see you. Who knows what they did with my letter.*

*I hope you find peace. My son Neal helped me pursue the matter
of payment with the insurance company. It's been an ordeal but
we've gotten some satisfaction, thanks to a review by an outside
agency. Enclosed is a check for the monies we owe you.*

Thank you for everything. God Bless.

Heyworth slipped the check into a desk drawer. He spotted his cur-
riculum vitae among the papers there. Constance had always kept it
updated. The document was twenty-three pages thick, and as he
thumbed it through, he remembered the wrought-iron balcony of the
hotel in Madrid where he addressed a group of Spanish doctors; the
medical film he'd shot with Dr. Hugh McGill, his surgical mentor; the
training he'd gotten and the medical societies to which he belonged.

On his computer screen, another of his dense scientific papers was
taking shape. When he finished this article, it would be the forty-first
he'd published. But now such papers spoke to him, not of his future, but
of his past, and he turned off his computer. That night, he slept better
than he had in days.

During his second week at home, Dr. Tolson came by in his scrubs.
His dark eyes had a familiar brooding look like when he had dropped by
Heyworth's office, or run into him in the doctors' lounge.

"You didn't hear the news today, I guess," Tolson said.

Heyworth was at the bar making gin and tonics for them. "I'm trying
to forget about what goes on at the hospital," he said. "No news. No
rumors. No gossip."

"Well, I've got to tell you this," Tolson said sitting his heavy frame on a bar stool. "The hospital is being merged with a larger company. They announced it this morning. The board apparently did it under duress. The acquirer says the hospital fits into their network and they're going to invest some capital and so on. Who knows, it might help things. It'll be in the papers tomorrow."

Heyworth handed Tolson a drink and raised his glass. "Cheers," he said. "To the future."

They clinked their glasses and drank.

Tolson wiped his moustache, energized by the thought of more news he had yet to tell. "I also heard Drew Shannon is out as medical director. I saw him in the hall just before I came here. He looked dejected, though he was trying mightily to keep up appearances."

"Let's go sit outside," Heyworth said. "The heat has broken, and it's tolerable now."

As the two men slipped through the sliding-glass door to the patio, Tolson was exulting over Shannon's downfall. "I heard he pleaded for his job, but apparently the new CEO has his own medical director in mind. Shannon will probably have the option to stay on the cardiology staff."

"Probably," Heyworth said as he relaxed into a deck chair.

"I heard the new owners are moving Shannon's wife to another hospital in their network. The infamous team will be broken up. But he'll land on his feet. Don't you worry."

"He put his life into that hospital," Heyworth said. "Into executing what he felt had to be done."

"A lot of people put their life into it. You did."

"I put my efforts into my patients and my research," Heyworth said. "Shannon won't be able to go back into cardiology full-time because he was in it just half-time. He's lost the feel for it. He'll probably wind up working for one of the insurance companies."

"Then I *really* feel sorry for him."

A gust scattered the cocktail napkins and Heyworth retrieved them. The two men chatted idly about Tolson's practice until there was a pause. Tolson leaned in toward Heyworth and said, "I feel bad for not getting over here to see you sooner."

"One thing I've realized the last few weeks is that I don't have many friends," Heyworth admitted.

"Are you handling things okay? I mean it's quite an adjustment for you. Maybe you should talk to someone to help smooth things over."

Heyworth had almost called Vanessa Stoy one morning the week before. "Everything's suddenly different," he said. "My wife is off on a journey of self-discovery in South America. My daughter's left home for college. I'm not a doctor anymore. I haven't even told my father about this though I'm going out to see him next week. "

Heyworth watched the faint light play on the slate roof. "Maybe I underestimated how hard it would be to leave my practice. At times, I feel like a part of me has died."

"Do you know what you're going to do?" Tolson asked.

"Probably get into some business. I don't know what yet. I've got a little capital and a bit of latent talent, I think. We'll see. In time, I'll find a long-term goal that holds my interest."

"Sometimes I wish I had your options."

"Sometimes I wish I had your youth," Heyworth replied.

Their drinks were empty and in the dark they could barely see one another's faces. Heyworth started to get up to turn on the porch lights but changed his mind.

"About a month ago," he confided, "my wife told me of her interest in another man. It's obvious I haven't paid enough attention to her needs. And I don't know why, except that I got out of the habit and I've been busy tending to my own needs and to the needs of my patients. I've got to get myself in a better frame of mind before she gets back, I know that."

Heyworth absently tried to sip from his empty glass. "I got out my wife's pasta machine a few days ago. I think I've perfected penne. The tubes even remind me a little of heart valves. You want to stay for dinner?"

"I need to get home," Tolson said, chuckling. "My wife is expecting me. And I'm late as usual."

The two men walked through the kitchen, out to the front door. As they headed down the stone walkway, Heyworth shook Tolson's hand.

"It means a lot to me, your coming here."

"I'll check on you later in the week, my friend," Tolson replied.

*   *   *

Heyworth left for San Belladro on Friday afternoon. West of Madsen, the land showed the first dry brown of autumn. After a four-hour drive, he stopped at the university campus to pick up Aline.

She came out of her dorm carrying an overnight bag and the beaded black purse Marge had given her as a going-away-to-college present. She wore a red, low-cut V-necked T-shirt over flared stretch-denim pants.

Heyworth smiled at the graceful, mature way she carried herself. It wasn't until Aline settled into the front seat that he noticed a metal nugget, the size of bee-bees, in each of her nostrils.

They drove out the old two-lane highway toward San Belladro. The rural road had many forks, twists, places to make a wrong turn. Behind grassy knolls, police cars lay in wait for unwary speeders.

"If you can wait for dinner," Heyworth said as they passed through a strip of fast-food restaurants, "we'll have a big meal at the ranch."

"That's fine. I had some cookie dough a while ago."

"Cookie dough?"

"My roommate eats a ton of it."

"Your mother would die."

"She doesn't have to know everything."

Aline was clearly savoring her independence, and Heyworth wondered about her life in the dorm. "You like your roommate?"

"She's not the smartest person I've ever met. She's very interested in boys and wants to pledge a sorority."

"And you're not interested?"

"Not in sororities."

"You're not the type," he said, looking at her appreciatively. "But what do the college boys say about that ring in your nostrils?"

"Any boy I'd like would like it."

"The tips there," he said pinching his septum, imagining the weight in his nose. "They look like steel boogers." Heyworth chuckled, and Aline tried not to smile but she gave in, and they laughed and went on laughing.

A few minutes later, she turned toward the side window, unscrewed the tiny balls in her nostrils, slipped off the connecting ring, and put it on the dash.

"Don't take that off on my account," he said.

"Oh, Grandpa won't like it either. I might as well get it over with. He's not going to like that beard you've got going there either."

"You're probably right."

The towns they passed looked forsaken, like scrub in a dry river bed. Stretches of empty road were relieved by a passing pick-up truck, a gas station. The trip was three hours—more time than they'd spent alone with each other, without distraction, in years. Along the way, Aline told him that during fall tennis training, she'd discovered the competition to earn a spot on the team as a walk-on was stiffer than she'd anticipated and would require serious, long-term dedication.

"Well, go for it, if you want it," he commented.

"I'm going to give it my best shot. I don't like to give up. Not without a struggle anyway."

As the sun went down, Aline dozed off. Heyworth grew groggy too, and he let one wheel of the car drift off onto the gravel shoulder. Aline woke up as he got the car squarely back on the road and sped on.

"There's something I need to tell you," he said, leaning on the arm-rest. "I've left my hospital practice."

She nodded as if the reason why he'd asked her to come along on the trip was dawning on her. "You didn't quit for Mother, did you?"

"This was my choice. My decision. But it might help us. We'll see." The glow of the car's dash made Aline's sharp-featured face look older. "There's a changing of the guard going on in medicine," he said, shoring up his explanation.

"I've always thought of you as a doctor."

"I spend a lot of time at home now, but you and your mother are both gone. It's odd how it's turned out." He focused on the road, the flat darkness ahead. "What would you think if Mother and I moved away from Madsen?"

"You don't have to stay there for me, if that's what you're asking."

"I don't know where we'd go, but I've begun considering our options."

Aline squirmed in her seat. "When I got your letter I thought you wanted me to come here this weekend so you could tell me that you and Mom were divorcing, or separating, or something along those lines."

"Oh, heavens," he said. "Did your mother imply that was coming?"

"No. But she's gone and I really didn't know what to think. I haven't heard from her. Have you?"

"She said she wasn't going to call for a while. Didn't she tell you that?"

"I guess I didn't believe her."

After another half-hour's drive, they turned off the highway onto a gravel road that led to Lloyd Heyworth's ranch house. Heyworth pulled the car up into the yard, under a stand of pine trees.

The wrap-around porch was spotted with dried mud. Behind the screen door, Lloyd stood watching, his eyes gray and deep-set, wearing a silk robe over low-heeled boots. The old man's posture was worsening. He seemed to be slowly curving inward, down toward the earth.

"Come in here," he said.

"What've you got there?" Heyworth replied, pointing at his father's metal cane.

"I call this my claw. It helps me get around." Lloyd lifted the tip of the cane like a branding iron and pointed inside the house as he bade them put their stuff in the back and get cleaned up for dinner.

The back rooms were drafty, the beds covered with old quilts Heyworth's mother had stitched. Aline went to the bathroom, and Heyworth stopped in the hallway.

On the plank wall was a framed photo of him and his brother, Jim. He was eleven, Jim, fifteen. Their cropped hair exaggerated Heyworth's sharp brow, Jim's plump cheeks and the silvery braces in his smile.

After their mother had died last year, Jim hadn't come to San Belladro for the traditional Thanksgiving dinner. Heyworth missed those days of togetherness and warmth when their families had been reunited.

Aline came up behind him, and they went to the kitchen where Lloyd waited. Behind him, a woman emerged from a room near the back door. She wore a drab dress but her skin was a vibrant honey-brown.

"This is Conchita," Lloyd said. "She drives out to check on me periodically and she's a darned good cook. I wanted tonight's meal to be special."

They gathered at the long pine table, and Lloyd sat at the head as though presiding.

"Dear God," he said, his voice craggy as he began a prayer. He liked Old Crow whiskey and swore, yet he went to Sunday school where the old men took turns giving sermons. "We thank you for our family and for our many blessings—" His blue lips quivered as his head dropped. As he'd gotten older, he was more emotional each time family gathered.

Heyworth looked up. "Thank you. Amen," he said.

The three of them ate the ham, sliced tomatoes, peas and corn bread and drank cold tea with limes in it sliced cross-grain in the Mexican way. As the meal progressed, Lloyd said he wanted to drive up to Bollinger tomorrow. Heyworth told him they'd go first thing in the morning. As Conchita brought refills, Lloyd began an old family story that Heyworth and Aline had heard him tell a half-dozen times over the years.

"I remember when Aline told me she wanted a pair of cowboy boots for her fifth birthday," Lloyd began, looking at her. "I found a pair at a farm-supply store in town. But when I gave them to you, you didn't like them. 'No, no, Grandpa,' you said, 'I want boots like this.'" He made a triangle with his fingers and looked with proud wonderment at Heyworth. "She wanted pointed toes on her boots. Not the square-toed ones I'd gotten her. And I got them for her, too. The very next week."

Aline smiled politely at her grandfather. "I still like cowboy boots, you know. Mom got me some last year."

"What are you studying, young lady?" Lloyd asked, glad to be sharing with family. "I was a biology major from the start. Always knew I wanted to be a doctor. Your father was the same way."

"I'm not that set on anything," Aline said, looking down at her plate. "I want to explore."

Heyworth knew Aline wasn't interested in medicine. He wasn't sure he'd encourage her even if she was. But he kept this to himself because his father viewed the family's heritage of medicine like land being passed down. "She's trying to get a spot on the tennis team," Heyworth said. "I admire her for that."

After dinner, Lloyd sat in his favorite chair watching TV half-asleep while Heyworth and Aline poured the black-and-white chess pieces on the dining table and arranged them on the board. It was the first time they'd played any game together in many years. After forty-five minutes, Aline's queen and a rook had penetrated Heyworth's defense. "I've got you," she said, her forehead ridged with determination.

"If I'd known you were this good at chess, I'd have insisted that we play checkers or backgammon."

"I played some in eighth and ninth grade and on the Internet, too, lately."

Heyworth stared at the board, his lip protruding. "Want to go to Bollinger with grandfather and me tomorrow?"

She didn't look up from the chess board.

"You could ride one of the horses if you want to stay here."

"I'll go with you," Aline finally said. "I might like that."

The next morning the sky was filled with low clouds that blew by quickly. Heyworth and Aline were dressed in jeans, but the old man had on a sport coat and one of his monogrammed dress-shirts. After Conchita made a breakfast of eggs with salsa, they headed north into what looked like nowhere. The sharp, red-clay terrain seemed wind-burned and raw. The car's tires hummed as they sped over the coarse gray asphalt.

When they'd driven beyond the ridge that led to the next plateau, Heyworth looked over at his father. "I'm leaving medicine. In fact, I've already turned in my resignation. It's been several weeks now, but I wanted to tell you in person."

Lloyd had a way of using silence to communicate. He looked ahead with no expression.

Two jackrabbits darted across the road. Aline pointed at them, leaning forward into the space between the front seats. She put her hand on her grandfather's shoulder. "Dad has made a hard choice, don't you think, Grandpa?"

"I love the science of medicine and the patients and surgery," Heyworth explained. "But so many of the other aspects of my practice have worn me down. Too much of the joy was gone out of it."

"Maybe you're too stubborn," Lloyd said. "Your mother said you were like that mule we had named Brutus."

"I remember Brutus," Heyworth said. For all the similarities between him and his father, there was a vast difference between the medicine he'd practiced in Madsen and the medicine his father had practiced years ago in the countryside.

Aline shifted in the back seat. Heyworth felt self-conscious explaining himself.

"My dissatisfaction built slowly," he said. "I had an exciting practice compared to some other doctors. I thought I was managing, but my unhappiness at work started to affect my self-esteem and my marriage, too. I was in a permanent state of conflict. It seeped into every facet of my life. Even into my spirit."

"What about your research?" the old man asked.

"I'm phasing out of that, too." Heyworth gripped the steering wheel tighter with both hands. "There was a case with a patient who in my judgment was not getting the proper treatment from another doctor. For me, that case crystallized how difficult things had become. I need to act on my judgment unencumbered by others. But that freedom is vanishing in medicine."

"Watch yourself," Lloyd grumbled. "You'll go into a depression. I did when I left my practice, and I didn't retire until I was almost seventy."

"I'll go through some of that, I'm sure. I already have, in fact."

After a long silence, Aline leaned forward and kissed her grandfather's cheek and then her father's, in quick succession.

"Thank you," Heyworth said over his shoulder.

They drove into Bollinger, a tiny town with no warning of its approach. Off to the left, a narrow white church sat on a cinder-block foundation. Heyworth parked and the three of them walked together to the cemetery. A short way down the path, Lloyd pointed with his cane to a tombstone. It was made of thin, course granite and tilted forward into the high grass so that the name on it couldn't easily be read.

"For years, my grandfather had one of those little gravestones like that," he said. "It was all that my grandmother could afford. But as I prospered, I upgraded the tombstones. Now our family's graves are the finest in this cemetery."

Farther along the footpath, the three of them faced the square mausoleum that held Lloyd's father, Heyworth's grandfather. It was stately, almost as big as a car.

"He was a great man," Lloyd said. The pouches of flesh below his eyes glistened with moisture.

"He died when you were just a year old," Heyworth explained to Aline, who nodded solemnly, her hands clasped at her waist. "He had cancer."

At the head of the mausoleum, Lloyd sat on the white granite bench and stared at the etching on the tomb's fascia. "When I was a boy," he said, beginning another story, one that neither Heyworth nor Aline had heard, "Daddy and I were out in a field one day. I was riding a horse behind him, and he came back to me and said, 'Son, there is no Santa Claus. You're going to discover that's a lie. But there is a God and that is not a lie.'"

Heyworth gripped his father's arm. They crested the knob of the hill, stopping at a spot that caught the morning sunlight and fronted the grave of Claire Heyworth. It was a wide, white-granite mausoleum that Lloyd had settled on for both his wife and himself.

Heyworth hadn't visited his mother's grave since her funeral last summer. He thought of her influences in his life: the soft quilt he'd slept under last night, the pillow he'd kept in his office that read, "Maybe in error, never in doubt," the sewing lessons she given him when he was a boy which he had put to good use during his years in medicine. Aline's competitive grit even reminded him of her perky spirit.

"It seems like she's been gone ten years. Five at least," Lloyd said.

"Hers is the only funeral I've ever been to," Aline said.

Lloyd lingered until his emotion was spent. When Aline began walking back to the car, he turned and followed her down the path.

At the ranch house, Conchita made Heyworth and Aline sandwiches for their return trip. They had to leave early so Aline could get back to her studies. When they were about to leave, Lloyd came out on the porch carrying a thin, square package wrapped in brown paper. He handed it to Heyworth. Inside was a picture of his mother—she was on the back patio, clutching her worn copy of Wordsworth's *Leaves of Grass*, standing near her hummingbird feeder. The picture had sat for years on Lloyd's dresser. After her funeral last year, Heyworth had commented how well it captured her.

Aline offered to drive on the way back, which made Heyworth squirm inititally because he wasn't in control. The afternoon was sunny, brilliant.

"That was a nice visit," Aline said. "I enjoyed it. A lot more than I thought I would."

Her nose ring was still on the dash. Heyworth picked up the tiny metal balls and the delicate curved pin and handed it to her. When they came to a straight stretch of road, she used her knee to steer the car and fastened the ring into place.

"Better," he said when she looked over at him.

"Okay," she replied. "I'm surprised Grandpa didn't see this. It was sitting here the whole time on our trip to the cemetery."

"He probably didn't know what it was."

It was quiet for a long time as they drove. Then Heyworth pressed on into the crease of intimacy he'd carved out with her during the last two days. "Your mom and I are having problems. Obviously."

"Yeah."

"But I want her and me to stay together. And I want you and me to be closer too."

"We are already," Aline said.

"I had fun with you this weekend. More than I have in a long, long time. We should do it again."

"Sure."

They crossed over shallow rivers and tributaries as they neared the university. At the campus, Heyworth got out Aline's overnight bag, and though it was not heavy, he carried it to her dorm. She didn't invite him in, but while students went in and out of the door behind them, she hugged him, holding him for a long time.

On his long drive back to Madsen, the sun was setting in Heyworth's rearview mirror, and he thought of how important his father's blessing was to him and how he'd connected at a deeper level with his daughter. For the first time in months, he felt the swell and rise of possibility.

As he came east, he saw the familiar outlines of the city and the downtown skyscrapers and the tall towers of the medical center. He imagined his old office and his desk and the view out his window and his crammed bookshelves and the gurneys in the hallways and the sign over the door of his operating room that read, "Quiet please, heart sleeping." The city's tendrils enveloped him, and then there was a jittery tremor in his stomach that was a longing to get away from the world he was going back to. "It will never be the same here for you," he thought as he sped on.

*   *   *

Two weeks later, on the day of Marge's return to Madsen, a storm blew through and afterward the sky cleared. Everything seemed rinsed. At dusk, Heyworth drove to the airport, arriving early so he'd be at the gate when she came through customs.

In the last few days, he'd regularly checked his messages, hoping she'd phoned. She'd finally called two nights before from a hotel at Iquitos, in the Peruvian jungle. She'd filled him in sketchily about her trek and then had asked about the FBI scare. Their phone connection went bad before they hung up, just as he was saying over the static, "Things are different around here."

At the terminal, Marge came through the gate carrying a straw basket with canvas rolls and brushes protruding. Her face was deep brown from the sun at high altitudes.

"You have a beard." She rubbed his cheek and hugged him. Then he took her bags and started up the concourse.

"How was your trip?"

"Good. Really good. Transforming, even."

They loaded the bags into the car and headed toward the skyscrapers of Madsen.

"The hiking in that altitude pulled things out of me that I didn't think I had," Marge said. "We went up into the mountains and then down to the jungles in the Amazon and then back up the mountains. I got sick from the thin air and the food and the water. But not too sick."

"What about your painting?"

"I've made a start. I did some drawings of the mountains and when I got back to Cuzco, I bought some paint."

The traffic was heavy on the beltway. They sat staring ahead at a line of cars that were merging into a single lane.

"I've got news," Heyworth said as the car inched forward. "I've left my practice."

"You have?" She looked sideways out the window. "I should have known by your beard. Actually I did know. You gave away your surprise."

"I feel more in control of my life. But there's a hole in it right now. I'm trying to look at this as an opportunity to grow."

"I'm all for that. We could both stand to grow."

They drove past boxy chrome and glass buildings, the clutter of stores and signs and lights, and then pulled into off into Morningside. The leaves on the trees were beginning to wither.

"It seems like I've been gone forever," Marge said.

"So long that it seems like we've been separated."

"We've traveled miles. I have literally."

He studied the side of her face. "I've wondered what you thought about while you were doing all that hiking."

They turned into the driveway before Marge could answer. At the back door, Cab ignored Heyworth, barking excitedly and pawing at Marge. Heyworth had dinner ready—penne cooked earlier that afternoon. They sat on the patio wearing light sweaters and made small talk over the flickering candles on the table. Heyworth told Marge about his trip with Aline to visit his father.

When Marge began gathering the dishes, Heyworth reached for her arm. "Sit back down a minute," he said. "I'll do that in a bit."

Marge rested her head against the chair, mesmerized by the lights in the swimming pool. Heyworth saw she was tired but weeks of worry over their relationship had built up in him.

"I know you just got back," he said. "But how are you? Really?"

"I fantasized a bit on my trip."

"Any of it you want to share with me?"

"I had time to look back and reassess. That's what I mean. That's a better way to put it."

"You said before you left that your life was shifting. What I'm wondering is how far you're going to shift and how I'm going to fit in."

"You've shifted too, David. At least when you practiced medicine, I knew who and what you were. It's as if there are new parts of you that I've yet to see."

"I know. But I'm only just discovering this myself," he said. "So did this trip help you find out who you were?"

"I didn't have any aha's, if that's what you mean. It doesn't seem to work like that. I'm just trying to get in touch with my deeper needs. It's a process." Marge wiped her mouth with a napkin. "But I've thought about our relationship a lot. I feel I'm in a place where I can make a better effort. Are you? Sometimes I feel skeptical about it, David."

"I've been through the worst of the withdrawal of leaving medicine. That will help. So I won't be such a bear."

He moved his hand across the glass table, and she clasped his fingers tightly.

"Speaking of getting us in a place to make a better effort, I've been thinking about us moving away," he said, his tone lighter. "That's been one of my fantasies, I'll admit."

"Mine, too."

"Seriously? You've been thinking about that?"

"I've been thinking about that for years, David. You just didn't know it."

"Really?"

"Really. Now, where would you like to go? What are your ideas?"

"What about San Belladro? We could even move into Dad's house until we found a place." He knew she'd reject this suggestion but offer another. "He's getting to where he needs someone with him," he added.

"If we're going to live on a ranch, let's go somewhere like Wyoming. We talked about doing something like that when we first met."

"It was a dream," he said. "Wyoming is far away. But fun to think about."

"Oh, it's blue-cold in the winters out there anyway." Marge's eyes were bright against her bronzed skin. She gave a smile with a spark of impulse behind it. "But I could paint the mountains there. The east side of the Tetons. We could build a cozy cabin with space for a studio."

"You're not the cabin type," he said, "and neither am I."

"You're the one who's soft. I just slept in a tent for a month. Ate bad food." Her imagination was stirred. She titled her head up at the pin lights in the trees. "We could ski out there seven months of the year if we wanted to."

"Just think of the glorious summers and the autumn," he said. "The ever-loving lack of humidity."

"We could both do and be something new."

"Together," he said.

She turned to him, looking serious. "It's not going to be easy for us, David. It'll take time and effort."

"I realize that. Believe me."

After they cleaned the dishes, Marge went to unpack, and he followed her to the bedroom. He watched her through the passageway as she washed her hands and put lotion on her sunburned face. She came to the bed and sat by him, smelling fresh. He gently pulled the towel off her shoulders and caressed her cheek with his hand.

They embraced, pushed her luggage off the bed, and lay back. They kissed and rolled over, pulling tighter, and undressed and touched. When they were finally still she had her hand across his chest, and he put his arm around her and they closed their eyes. She imagined the mountains with snow and sharp light on them and he visualized wide-open spaces as they drifted off to sleep.